ONCE BITTEN TWICE TURNED

Eva Peony

ISBN-13: 9798779479646

Cover design by: Art Painter
Library of Congress Control Number: 2018675309
Printed in the United States of America

To all who feel lost.

PART ONE

CHAPTER ONE

The sound of the music reverberates from my toes to my head, sending an electrifying shiver down my spine. It has been two years since the world turned chaotic, two years since I last saw a band live, two years since anything truly made sense.

Everyone just works as if that were all that can be done. I'm sick of working, sick of having to rush home to make curfew of having to spend whatever time remains a slave to the system.

Ma believes it'll get better; I say it'll only worsen.

Someone taps my shoulder. The acrid stench of cigarette smoke clings to the stranger. The smell amplified the moment he leaned down to whisper in my ear, "wanna go have some fun?" the stranger's raspy voice made me think of a dog with a bad cough.

I take a step back, bumping my back against someone's shoulder, "Sorry, not interested," I say, turning to apologize to the person I bump into. A girl with cat-like eyes smiles at me, but she hisses when the stranger tries to reach for me. The man's eyes widen, uncertainty filling his slightly glossed-over eyes.

"Who sent you?" the girl asks, but the stranger doesn't get to answer as he starts to convulse.

The girl lets out a sigh before taking my hand and pulling me through the crowd. "You don't want to be caught," she says as the sea of people part for us. Someone notices the convulsing man. Next thing you know, everyone is trying to get out.

Concerts, like most things, are currently forbidden; the Enforcers will show up soon and lock everyone up. We make it outside just in time to duck into an alley the bands already loaded up.

"You two want a lift?" the drummer asks.

"I'm good," I say, breaking free of the girl's hold, "thanks."

"To him or me?" the girl asks.

"Both," I walk past the band's van and duck into a separate alley. Having decided I no longer care if I live or die. I've taken it upon myself to learn the city's ins and outs, like all the shortcuts and even the entrance to the Forgotten City.

As I'm about to make the final turn, something pulls me back, sharp pain spreading from my throat to my heart. Something like claws digs into my abdomen and shoulder, my vision blurs as my knees go weak. The last thing I remember is the taste of something metallic flooding my mouth and dripping down my throat.

Something nips at my shoulder while something else digs into my ribs. I open my eyes to the loveliest moon I have ever seen. The moonlight calls to me, pulling me towards her. I somehow climb out of the ditch I'm in. Where am I? I topple over my foot, catching on a root.

When I reach down, the pain in my ribs intensifies. I reach back and pull out two wooden daggers. Something runs through the shrubbery before I can question how I got here, triggering something within.

I close my eyes and inhale, my senses overwhelmed by the sound of wolves howling, of songbirds and owls hooting. Most importantly, by the beating hearts and pulsing blood, I track the tiny creature and, without hesitation, sink my fangs in. Warmblood pools in my mouth; I don't stop until the little creature stops fighting.

Something is watching me, but I do not care; the hunger consumes me. I need more. Following the sound of sleeping hearts, I stumble upon a farm. Without a second thought, I drain the cattle, the chickens, the pigs. Even the farmer that gets in my way. Would it be wrong for me to say I feel no remorse?

With my hunger sated, I head back into the forest; those eyes continue to follow my every move. But I do not care; perhaps I'll have dessert. Footsteps, no paw steps near me, and as I turn, something knocks me to the ground. Warm fur graces my fingers tips.

I try to throw the wolf off me, but somehow, he's more powerful. The wolf sinks his canines into my shoulders. Causing me to let out a growl of disapproval. Before my eyes, I watch as the wolf transforms into a man. His golden-brown eyes burn with a question, "Who are you?" and a command "stay down."

"Well, this is interesting," a female voice says, "it seems there was no saving you."

There is a familiarity to her when the male climbs of me. I look up to emerald cat eyes. The male takes the jeans and boots; she hands him.

"I'm Mika," she extends her hand towards me, "what's your name?"

"Lilith," I say, surprised at the change in my voice, "What am I?"

"Vamp," the male growls out, "a reckless one at that."

"Don't mind, Sean," Mika says, "he dislikes everything and everyone."

Standing I dust myself off, Sean's bite seems to have given me a sense of clarity, "Where am I?" I ask the easier of the two questions. Did I really kill that man?

Sean seems to know what I'm thinking; he takes a step towards me, leaning down, he whispers, "yes."

Something about how he utters that one word has me inching to fight him. How was I supposed to know what I was doing? I raise my hand, but he catches it midway, "Be careful little vamp, or tonight might be your last night."

Mika steps between us, forcing Sean to let go; he shakes his head as he walks away midnight hair swaying in the moonlight. "Don't mind my brother; he lacks certain sensors."

Brother, I look from Mika to Sean while there is a resemblance. I can't help but say, "but you're a cat."

Sean sneers while Mika giggles, "our mother has a thing for shifters and the such; we also have a brother that's a lion and one that's a crow. Actually, I'm more of a yokai, to be precise a bakeneko."

"I don't know what that means," I say.

Mika smiles as she starts to guide me towards her brother, "I'm not surprised," she says, "our myths, much like yours, are rarely explored."

Mika leads me towards a black SUV while Sean trails behind us, a Crow rest atop the roof; he flaps his wings and flies towards us. Shifting as he lands, a hauntingly beautiful Male stands before me. His eyes remind me of amethyst encased in silver like Sean and Mika; his hair is midnight black. His skin is only slightly fairer than Sean's. At the sight of his brooding brother Crow snickers.

"What's the matter," Crow twirls a strand of my muddy hair, "brother, the two of you just met, don't tell me you already plan on claiming her."

"You think I'm some Fay bastard that…

Before Sean can finish his sentence, a roar cut's him off.

Mika leads me around her brothers and into the SUV, "Try growing up with three insufferable bastards," she shuts the door behind me and climbs into the driver's seat. Sean takes shotgun, and Crow settles beside me.

"That roar?" I ask as something taps my shoulder. I turn to find a lion curled up in the back, his paw resting on my shoulder, "you weren't kidding."

Mika laughs while the lion pats my shoulder. Crow snickers as I watch with amazement as yet again, someone transforms before me. A golden light emanates from the lion, and then there's only a sleepy-looking Male.

"I'm Leo," he extends his hand towards me, "mom has a sense of humor," Leo adds, at my confusion.

I turn to Crow and ask, "So then are you, Crow?"

He responds by laughing, "you can call me whatever you want," he leans in and flicks my chin.

"Rafael!" While soft, Mika's voice holds enough command to get Crow to sit back on his side of the truck, "ignore them all."

The rest of the drive passes by in silence until a thought hit's me, "how did I end up in that ditch?"

"The Vamp that turned you shouldn't have been hunting in your city," Leo says, "wannabe hunters caught up to him. After he got away, they took you out of the city; the wooden daggers didn't go in deep enough to kill you."

"You know all this, how?" I ask as anger rises.

"Rafael was able to track you through your energy imprint," Mika says, "it's been four days; your family believes you dead. For them and for yourself, it's best if it remains that way."

"Four days," I say more to myself, "wait, why were you tracking me?"

Sean looks at me through the rear-view mirror, "Mika made us; she can sense when somethings off."

Even if she can sense when something is off, what's it to her? "That's all you're going to say?"

"What else would there be?" Sean sneers; it seems to be his favorite expression.

"Ama might be able to help you," Mika says.

"As long as you haven't had mortal blood, you should be fine," Leo adds. At my frightened look, he leans in, sniffing my throat, "oh, you're screwed."

CHAPTER TWO

We pull up to a gray stone just in time to avoid the rising sun. Not thinking, I open the door and scream the moment the first rays of sunlight hit my skin. Rafael pulls me back, cloaking me with his hoodie.

"Foolish girl," he mutters, "you can't go out that way."

Since my head is covered, I can't see where I'm headed, but at least Rafael doesn't let go. I can feel myself going down as if on a slide, and then the hoodie's pulled off me.

"You can sleep down here," Mika says, "I'll let Ma know," she takes her cat form and sprints past us.

"Where am I?"

"Our home," Rafael says, "well technically, you are below it."

"The Forgotten City."

"Part of it," Sean opens the door to a dark room, "the area below our home and above is neutral territory."

"Why?" I step through the threshold, my eyes adjusting to the welcoming darkness.

"Ama's a Healer," Leo says, "all territory occupied by Healers is considered neutral."

"Not everyone respects that," a female appears, Mika by her side, "Where did you get burned?"

I extend my hand; the skin is still slightly burned. Warm light engulfs me as the burning across my face stops. How did I not realize I burned my face?

"You had a light sensitivity before, didn't you?" the Female asks.
How did she know, "Yes, why?" I respond.
"Whether you consider this a gift or a curse, know that you are not only stronger and faster, but your light sensitivity has increased. As you grow older, it should get better, but it'll never go away."
"Is there a way to undo what I've become?" I ask while trying to fight the sleep that's trying to claim me.
"Rest, there's no use in fighting it," the Female leads me towards the bed, "we'll talk when you wake."
I nod my agreement and collapse on the bed. My dreams are filled with images of blood and screams. At some point, I dream of a male with skin as cold as ice, eyes as red as rubies, and hair as white as snow. He calls out to me, and while lovely, something about him repels me.
The last thing I truly want is to be near him. Something sinister lurks behind his feral smile. The strange Male tries to reach for me, and the moment I take a step back, I fall. The world spirals out of control, and then just like that, I'm flying higher and higher.
"Isn't it lovely?" a songlike voice asks; when I try to turn, he stops me, "just look at the sleeping city; it doesn't compare to you."
"Who are you?" I ask, but he just chuckles, and then there's darkness. I wish he hadn't left me.
Finally, when I wake, I find the room I'm in glows. It's as if the walls were made of iridescent stone. There's a soft pink glow coming from what I find to be the bathroom. Without a second thought, I strip and step into the shower.
Muddy water pools at my feet before it's all whisked away by the drain. I scrub my skin until the dried blood starts to fall off. Realizing I have nothing to clean myself, I step out of the shower, water still running. A shelf is carved into the wall where washcloths and bath towels are folded neatly.
I take one of the washcloths and step back into the shower. There's a rose-scented shampoo and conditioner along with a strawberry-scented body wash. I scrub my face first, then the rest of me. Enjoying the feel of the water on my skin, I take my time washing my hair.

Even from here, I can hear footsteps approaching; rinsing out the conditioner, I step out of the shower and head towards the towel shelf. Water pools around me, more falling to the floor as I ring out my hair. Will I have this hairstyle forever? I guess it's a good thing I waxed before leaving the house that night.

But, can I really not see my family ever again? There's a light knock on the door, "Lil, are you awake?" Mika asks.

Wrapping myself in a dry towel, I walk out of the bathroom and open the bedroom door. Crow sits on her shoulder; he lifts a wing as if to hide his face.

"What's he's deal?" I step back so Mika can walk in.

"He's being shy," Mika hands me a bundle of clothes, "this should fit, oh, and Ma sent you spiced blood."

I take the clothes and coffee thermos, "Spiced blood?"

Crow takes that moment to shift, "she added cinnamon to it and a few coffee grounds."

"So, it's a Bloody Coffee?" I ask, seating the clothes down. I open the thermos, a sweet aroma wafting out.

"I guess you could call it that," Crow takes a seat on the lounge chair.

"Why are you here?" I ask before taking a sip of the warm blood.

"How is it?" Mika asks.

Ignoring her, I drink every last drop wishing there was more. Crow gets up and yanks the thermos from my hands, "here," he says as the blood on the sides and bottom connects and hovers out in a sphere-shaped drop. I open my mouth, and he lets it fall in, "I'd say she likes it."

"More," I reach for him, and before I can sink my fangs in, I'm frozen in place.

"I'd prefer you didn't feed on my children," their mom stands by the doorway, arms crossed, a bemused look on her face, "get dressed and meet us upstairs."

With that, Crow's dragged out of the room; Mika doesn't look my way as she closes the door.

We head down an archaic corridor. Torches line the walls red, blue, and green flames dance on either side, a stone gate parts for us, and suddenly we're in a modern basement. Sean and Leo sit in front of a massive flat-screen game controller in hand; chips and popcorn are scattered everywhere.

I never thought immortals set around playing video games and eating popcorn. Sean jumps in excitement, and Leo snorts, "Lucky win."

"You're just mad you lost," Sean tosses popcorn into his mouth, "the great Leo isn't great at everything after all."

Leo picks up popcorn and tosses it at his brother, "shut up," he's about to throw a soda can when Mika clears her throat.

"Having fun?" their mother asks.

Leo shrugs, and Sean looks away; I guess even immortals fear their mothers.

"It's nice not to be the one in trouble," Crow whispers in my ear, sending a familiar thrill through me. I turn to look at him, and he shifts, flying to his sister's shoulder and tucks his head inside his wing.

"What's with him?" I ask.

Mika taps her brother's wing, "he's tired."

"We'll be upstairs," their mother says, "I expect this messed cleaned up," with that, she leads us up the stairs and into a brightly lit kitchen. Pots and pans hang from the ceiling, a tray of freshly baked cookies sits on the isle.

"You'll probably throw them up," Mika points for me to sit in one of the floral chairs.

"I almost forgot, call me Heather, "Mika's mom sets a cup of spiced blood in front of me, and I drink it without a second thought.

"Thank you," I wish Crow could collect the last drops of blood like before. As if hearing my thoughts, drops of blood start to float up until their one. I open my mouth and catch it as Crow peeks from under his wing.

"No magic on the dinner table," Heather takes Crow and sets him on a chair; he shifts back a bored look on his lovely face.

He leans back in his chair, head hanging sideways, "So boring," without warning, he reaches forward and wipes blood from the corner of my mouth, "don't be wasteful," he brings his thumb to his mouth and licks the blood away, "why can't I get spiced blood?"

Heather smacks him upside the head, "you're not a guest," she hands him a cookie and takes the remaining seat, "besides you only drink blood for the taste," she sets a plate of chocolate peanut butter cookies on the center of the table.

"Why would you drink blood?" I ask, to which he shrugs as he munches on his cookie.

"What would you like to know?" Heather asks.

Looking away from Crow, I ask, "who turned me?"

Heather lets out a little sigh, "that I don't know; there has been an increase in rogue Vamps throughout the Cities."

Mika cuts in, "it looks like they're looking to out all immortals."

"They're trying to take advantage of the supposed world's end," Heather says.

"You don't believe the world's ending?" I ask.

Heather shakes her head, "I've seen worlds end; this is nothing but a minor setback meant to teach people a lesson in human decency."

"What Ama's saying is, the earth is tired of all the pollution, wars, and the hate," Crow says, "the world's just trying to reset."

Mika reaches for a cookie, "Hopefully, all the racist fucks get taken out of the equation. Along with all the sadist."

"Unfortunately, the world requires a balance," Heather says, "to have good, you must have evil. To many, it's all perspective."

"Can I really never see my family again?" I ask before they can talk more about balance and the such.

"Unless immortals are exposed, you have to avoid them," Heather says, "it's best if you find a Clan to take you in."

"Clan?" I ask as I dig my nails into my palms.

"Vamps are divided into Clans or Houses, their kind of like tribes or packs," Crow says, "they believe in strength in numbers and have rules in place to keep you safe."

"I thought Vamps are loners," I can't take it anymore. I take a cookie, and not a second passes before I'm throwing it up.

"Best, she learns now," Heather hands me a dishtowel.

"Couldn't you throw up on Mika?" Crow asks.

"I didn't mean to," I say, just as Sean and Leo enter the kitchen. Sean starts laughing while Leo helps Crow clean himself off.

"You won't be able to eat," Leo says, "it's a blood-only diet for you."

"But I love bacon," I say, thinking of all the things I love to eat only makes me sad, as sad as knowing I'll never see my family again, "Is there no way of undoing this?"

"You could drink pigs' blood," Leo says sympathetically, "cows when you want a burger."

"I doubt it's the same," I say.

"Kill your Sire," Heather says, "granted you first have to know who Sired you."

CHAPTER THREE

How the hell am I supposed to find my Sire when I don't even know who turned me. I let out a sigh while tucking my head into my knees.

"What's wrong?" Crow asks.

I lift my head, "How will I find him or her?" the clouds hide the stars. Since the world started falling apart, it's easier to see the stars. Not the way you would in the country or mountains but still better than before.

"You're connected," he says, "just tug on that invisible thread."

I look towards him, "Why didn't your mother mention it?" I ask.

"She thinks it dangerous," he says, "just be happy you get a second chance."

"What's great about not being able to eat the things I like?"

Crow laughs, "I feel like you're more upset about not being able to eat than you are about not seeing your family."

"Somehow, I know they'll be fine," I stand and brace myself against the chimney, "so I just jump, and I'll land as graceful as a cat?"

Crow nods, "gravity will take over; it likes our kind," without another word, he jumps. I take an unnecessary breath and jump. The distance from the roof to the garden isn't great, but I'm still surprised when I land gracefully.

"Told you, gravity loves us," he jumps up, landing on the garage roof; I follow after him, and soon we're hopping from rooftop to rooftop until we're high up in the trees.

"You said, us?" I ask when we stand atop the remnants of a library. "Immortals," he says, "if you had gone with Sean, he would have showoff."

I snicker, "because you're not," I jump down my hood, staying in place.

Crow lands beside me, "he thinks he's alpha just because he beat his old man, trust me. I'm holding back."

"Why doesn't he like you?" I ask, not looking as I cross the street. "Don't be reckless."

"We just got here by jumping on rooftops; how is this reckless," I stop mid-street and raise my hands.

He shakes his head and pulls me onto the sidewalk, "my father and his don't get along. For whatever reason, Sean believes we have to be like them."

"You should tell her the whole truth," Sean jumps down a building, eyes glowing.

"You mean how your old man wanted mother to choose him," Crow mocks, "but she instead chose my father."

"He's just like him," Sean says, "he'll use you, then leave you."

Crow lets out a mocking laugh, "mother knew what my father was long before he bedded her. But what did your father want," he taps his chin, "oh, that's right, a whore. The bastard has a Mate, but he chased after mother, almost getting her killed."

"Enough!" I can't take their bickering anymore, "Do you think it wise to argue about family matters out in the open. Don't you know the winds always listening?" not waiting for a response, I walk away from them.

The stench reaches me before the person those, "Hello, pretty lady, how would you like to be with a real man?"

I tilt my head to the side, a strand of mauve hair slipping out, "I would love to, do you know any?" without wasting time, I reach for the man, claws sinking into his throat "you pestered me that night. Tell me where your master is?"

The filthy bastard claws at my hand, trying to break free. His blood has the pungent stench of cigarette smoke and decay. Drinking his blood would be like drinking shit. Crow and Sean run up to me, halting behind me.

Sean lets out a growl, "put him down."

I let out a manic laugh, "I'm not a hound, I don't have to listen to you," I say, snapping the stranger's neck, my grip severing his head, "here, a present for you," I toss the body at Sean and walk away.

Crow trails behind me; not a peep escapes him. He leads me into an alley and magics the blood away.

His silence is killing me, "Say it," I say.

He just looks at me, his eyes betraying nothing.

"Cro... Rafael, say something."

He gives me a smile, "what did you say?"

I roll my eyes, annoyed at him and the world, "Say something."

Crow brushes a loose strand of hair behind my ear, "before that."

"Rafael."

"No," he tilts his head sideways, "before that, you stopped yourself."

I bite my tongue, warm blood pooling my mouth, "Crow."

He gives me a wicked smile, "only you can call me that," he pulls his hand away, "I know a place you might like."

Crow takes me down another alley then through a secret passage into the tunnels. Within minutes we stand outside a club, a glowing red moon its only insignia. We walk past the line and straight up the steps; the door opens for us, closing with a loud thud when we cross the threshold.

"Welcome to Red Moon," Crow lifts his hands up, "one of the few places where we don't have to pretend to be mortal."

The interior has a red glow; the balcony windows are shaped like red crescent moons. A Faun runs past us bells dangling from her horns, a very drunk centaur chasing after her.

"So, all myths are true?" I ask as Crow guides me towards the bar.

He nods at the bartender whose skin glows under the dim lights, "Most, hey Serpentine."

The bartender nods at us, the light making his eyes look reptilian, "Your, usual?"

"Surprise me," Crow says. Serpentine looks my way before I can refuse. Crow speaks, "she likes sweets."

Serpentine starts mixing drinks; he sets an amethyst drink in front of me and an emerald one in front of Crow.

"Trust me," Crow takes a swing of his drink, not bothering to taste it. I pick mine up and pray I don't throw it up. The cocktail has hints of citrus and lavender; without the blood, will it stay down. I take another sip, and before I know it, I've finished it.

"Want another?" Serpentine asks.

"Yes," I say, earning a smile from Crow.

"For whatever reason, Vamps have no trouble digesting liquor," Crow says, "it's just the solids."

"So, should I puree my food?" I ask.

A pretty female with lime green eyes approaches us, "I'd advise against that," She's like a fiery sunrise with her curly hair, a mixture of red and orange. "I'm Mia," she extends her hand.

"You're a Vamp," I take a step back.

"I am," she tucks her hand away, a smile on her pretty face, "what clan do you belong to?"

"I…

"Lilith's new," Crow interrupts, "that's why we're here."

"The rare survivor," Mia nods as if remembering something within the blink of an eye; another Vamp stands beside her.

He looks me over, silver eyes scrutinizing as if finding what he needs; he nods, "We'll take her," the man says.

I turn to Crow, "what is this?"

Crow lets out a sigh, "we told you, you need a clan. Mia's a friend, so is Cyrus; it's best if you go with them."

"And if I refuse?" something within urges me to fight, yet part of me wants to believe Crow knows what he's doing.

"You'll die," he says, all nonchalant, "now be a good girl and go with them."

"No," I turn to leave, but something holds me in place. There's pressure in my head as if something was trying to pry it open. Remembering what I've read about Vamps and Fay, I start to build walls, blocking them out until I can move.

"She's strong," Cyrus says.

Crow snorts, "she's stubborn."

"You are worse than Sean," I say before walking off towards the entrance; I push past dancing couples and out the door. The wind blows my hood back strands of mauve hair breaking free. Closing my eyes, I start to run in no particular direction.

Fool, you just met. Why should Crow care about you? They're just trying to save their own skin.

I somehow end up before Lake Michigan, the waves barely breaking the surface. Not caring who hears me, I let out a scream. Like a petulant child, I stomp my feet and throw myself on the wet sand. "Why?" I shout into the night, "why couldn't I just die?"

CHAPTER FOUR

Ruby eyes greet me the moment I close my eyes, the coolness of the waves' seeps into my clothes, relaxing me as much as the sound of the waves. "Come to me," a sing-song voice murmurs. I sit up in time for the wind to blow water onto my face. Wet and frustrated, I rise.

The sing-song voice continues to call out to me. With nothing else to do, I start walking out of the water. There's the sound of hushed voices; I can hear them as clearly as if I was with them.

"Do you think she'll lead us to him?" a female voice asks.

"He Sired her," a male voice responds, "I'm certain of it."

"And if she can't?" another male asks.

"She's determined to undo what's been done," the first male voice says, "she'll find him."

"For how long will you string her along?" the female asks.

"As long as it takes to avenge Alexa," the first male responds.

So, he just wants to use me. Fine, two can play that game. What do I care for his revenge? For lying to me, I'll hold off on finding my Sire. After all, I never wanted to grow old; becoming a Vampire might just be what I needed.

As I walk down the shore, the sound of beating hearts awakens the hunger. Two figures are collapsed in the sand. A gasp escapes the female just as the aroma of sweet blood wafts over.

"What are you?" I ask.

The beautiful Male looks up as if surprised by my presence. Could he not pick up on my scent? He smiles, beckoning me to join him. "Aren't you lovely," blood drips down his chin and onto his exposed chest.

I kneel beside him and take the wrist he offers, "what's her crime?" He smiles a wicked glim in his emerald eyes, "she used her virtue to lure our kin to their deaths," he sinks his fangs back into her throat.

Closing my eyes, I bring the girl's wrist to my lips and bite. Her blood is sweeter than the farmers and tastes far better than the spiced blood Heather gave me. The Male lets out a laugh pulling me out of my thoughts.

"Stop," he commands, "my lovely, if you do not stop, you'll kill her. Can you live with that?"

I look up to find him leaning on his elbows, a different kind of hunger in his eyes.

"Yes," I say, surprising him when I move to the girl's throat and bite the already bloodied flesh.

He lets out another laugh before speaking, "I like your style," he launches at the female, sinking his fangs into her exposed flesh, and together we drain her of existence.

The Male gives me a pleased smile as I wash the blood away. With a wave of his hand, the girl turns to ash. Not even a trace of the blood she spilled remains as the waves wash it all away.

"What are you?" I ask.

"Typical American. Why ask my name? When you can ask what I am," he says, all nonchalant, "I'm a Vampire, like you."

"You have a heartbeat."

He leans down and starts washing his hands, "I used to be Fay; the change affects us differently."

I inch closer and ask, "so you can eat? I mean like actual food."

"Yes, little one," he says with a sigh, "I can eat actual food.

"Are there different breeds of Vampire?" I ask.

Droplets of water fall onto his toned chest like dewdrops; they trail down. I can only imagine where they'll lead, "of course, did your Sire not explain?"

"I don't even know who my Sire is," at my words, he stops scrubbing his face, "I didn't choose the change."

"I see," he wipes the blood off his chest and rises, brushing his trousers', "come with me."

"Why?" I take a step back, avoiding his outstretched hand.

"The sun will rise soon, and you're not old enough to fend it."

"But you are?" at my question, he pulls me towards him, and before I know it, we're running the city nothing more than a blur, and then we're inside a lavish Manor.

Vampires come and go, some stopping to greet us, others too busy to notice. That is until he sets me down at the center of the foyer.

"Welcome, I am Marcus, head of the Sanguis Clan," Marcus raises his hands to gesture at his home's grandeur, "my Sire had a sense of humor," he adds.

"Lilith," I say, avoiding the curious looks from all gathered.

"It seems your parents had a sense of humor as well," Marcus says, that wicked glimmer still in his eyes.

A Female Vamp approaches strawberry hair swaying with each step, "follow me," she takes my hand and starts pulling me towards the stairs, "I do wonder where my brother found you?" she asks as we reach the third landing.

"Where are you taking me?" I try to break free, but she's more powerful.

"The sun will be up soon," she says as if it was answer enough. We stop outside an oak door with a crescent moon carved into it. She opens the door and hands me the key, "this is your room."

I attempt to pull my arm free, but she's too strong, "Who says I'm staying?"

She lets out a little laugh, "Marcus would not have brought you here otherwise."

"He made a choice for me," I protest, "and how is he your brother?"

"I'll tell you another night, now take a shower while I find you some clothes," she throws me into the room and walks away, humming twinkle, twinkle, little star.

The room is surprisingly cozy, with a twin bed resting between two windows facing the door nightstands on either side. To my left are a computer desk and a work chair. Then to my right, a closet next to the bathroom. I close the door and head into the bathroom catching a glimpse of my reflection in the mirror.

I guess Vampires' lacking a reflection is a myth, or perhaps it varies by breed. As I look in the mirror, I realize my once amber eyes are now the fiery marigolds' color, orange-red at the center with a golden outline.

My waist-length hair is covered in blood and sand. Washing it all out should be fun. I strip off my sandy clothes and toss them into the hamper. Before walking into the shower, I make sure to find a washcloth and towel.

There are different bottles of shampoos and conditioners, from; coconut to strawberry, green apple, ocean breeze to rose, and citrus; the body washes follow the same range of scents. There's even a variation of exfoliants. What would Vamps need to exfoliate for? Picking the subtlest fragrance, I take the coconut shampoo, conditioner, and cocoa body wash. When I step out of the shower, a red nightgown is laid out on the bed.

"I figured we can go shopping tomorrow," the female walks in with a bundle of clothes she sets on the computer table, "Marcus doesn't like to go shopping; he'd rather order something online or have someone get it for him."

"What's your name?" I slip the nightgown over my head and pull the towel off as it falls right above my knee.

"Carmilla, I was named after a poem or something," she hands me a comb, "I forgot to set this in the bathroom."

"You bought all of those?"

"Marcus said someone was coming, and to prepare, it's just I didn't know your size, so I had to wait until I saw you."

"Marcus knew I was coming?"

"He can speak to us telepathically," Carmilla explains, "all Sires can do that, well actually anyone strong enough can. Now change and rest."

Before she can leave, I ask, "the windows?"

She smiles, "electric blinds, they'll descend ten minutes before sunrise. Marcus read about it in a book and had them installed. They're better than our old ones. Can't tear these open."

"I think I've read that book," I say just as the blinds start to descend, "wow."

"Sleep well," with that, I'm left alone.

Detangling my hair, I climb into bed, and sure enough, as the sun rises, I'm pulled into a deep sleep; at first, there is nothing, and then there is everything.

CHAPTER FIVE

I wake to the sound of knocking on my door; yet again, it takes me a moment to adjust. This is not my room; this is not my home. Groggily I crawl out of bed and open the door to a bemused Marcus.

"Sleep well?" he walks in without an invitation and sets a black bag on the bed, "Carmilla tells me you're going shopping."

Everyone keeps making decisions for me; I'm not a child. "She made that decision, not me," I don't move from my spot by the door. Instead, I watch as he inspects the clothes on the table.

"You shouldn't let her boss you around," he flips the lavender shirt over, "granted to her you're like a new toy. We rarely take in Vamps not Sired by me."

"Why?" I ask.

"Makes life easier," Marcus says.

"No, I mean, why am I like a new toy to her?"

Marcus leans against the computer desk, arms crossed, "your breed of Vampire normally belongs to Clans like Montana, Zarina, and Nosfera."

"Why are you pestering her this early at night?" Carmilla walks into the room, carrying a mug of steaming coffee, "try," she hands it to me as she turns to glare at Marcus, "shoo."

"I indulge you too much," he flicks her forehead before walking past me and out the door, "just remember whose money you spend."

"Like you ever let me forget," she turns to look at me, confusion in her eyes as I stare at the coffee, "what's wrong?"

"I don't know if I can drink this," I say, "when I tried to eat a cookie, I threw it up."

Carmilla snorts, "Marcus said there was poison in your system; he could smell it. That's why he shared his kill with you."

Poison in my system, "how is that possible?"

"Did you have anything besides the cookie?" she asks.

"An entire farm and spiced blood," I take a sip of the coffee than another until nothing remains.

When I don't throw up, Carmilla nods, "what's spiced blood?"

"Blood with seasonings, why?" I set the mug down on the computer table.

She seems to consider something before asking, "who gave you the blood?"

"Heather," I say, "she's a healer."

"Did you know her before you turned?"

"No, I met her after," I chew on my lower lip as I contemplate how much to say, "her children found me."

"Did you know them before the change?"

I shake my head, "oh, I met Mika right before I was turned at a concert."

"I need to check on something, get dressed, and meet me in the foyer," Carmilla runs out, the door closing with a light thud.

What would they gain by making me believe I can't eat? I walk over to the bed and pull-out black ankle boots and a black coat. Can Vampires get cold? At that thought, a voice whispers in my head, "you need to blend in."

"Get out of my head!" I shout masculine laughter, the only response.

I dress quickly and head downstairs; vampires run back and forth, some dressed in scrubs, others in suits, paramedic, and firemen uniforms.

"Yes," a male vampire says, "we have ordinary jobs; not everyone had the luxury of accumulating a fortune."

"I see, but how does it work," I nod towards one of the paramedics.

"They learned self-control long ago; I'm Luis, by the way," Luis extends his hand towards me, the action something I've only seen on old shows and movies. Oh, and at that bar, Crow took me to. The pandemic, twenty-five years ago, changed a lot of things.

After the virus, there were about four years of peace before the world went downhill. The ice caps melted, but at the same time, a meteoroid hit, taking out Texas and turning it into the icecaps. Due to e-learning, the schools turned to ruin, and most libraries. The majority of things could be accessed online.

Of course, two years ago, the Civil War broke out, the power went out, and the internet was shut down to control the masses. Now people just count the days until the end of the world. I wonder what it was like to live before the world went to hell without curfews and giant hornets.

Dammed scientists always messing with what they shouldn't. Made things worse when they tried to get rid of the killer hornets. There are also the mutated animals that were trapped in the zoo when a bomb went off. Whatever was used to make that bomb made the animals different, like the two-headed snakes and giant bats.

"Are you alright?" Luis asks.

"Sorry, it's just...

"Right, your generation just nods at people," Luis tucks his hand away, "where you off to?"

"I'm waiting for someone," I say, "what do you do?"

"I'm head of security," he looks down at his wrist and old watch ticking the time away, "I should get back to work, stay out of trouble."

"Okay," I look around and spot Carmilla arguing with a nerdy-looking mortal. Should I listen in? I mean, would they even know.

"Lilith," Carmilla ushers me forward, "this is Vincent, our tech. Could you describe the people you met when you first woke?"

"Why?" at closer inspection, the mortal isn't bad-looking.

"Carmilla has a theory, as do I," Marcus leans against a pillar. He now wears an immaculate black suit; his onyx hair is comb back, and a silver watch picks out of his sleeve.

"It was a family, a lion named Leo, a wolf named Sean," I chew my bottom lip, "a fay named Crow, and a cat named Mika. They said their home is neutral territory."

Marcus has a deadly silence to him, while Carmilla looks like she might kill someone. Vincent, I realize, was typing everything I said into his flat screen.

"Is this them," he holds up the screen images of the siblings and their mother.

"That was fast," I say, catching the slightest hint that Marcus is bothered by my confirmation, "Rafael took me to see Mia; he wanted me to join her Clan."

Marcus snorts, "if, by clan, he means her incest pool, sure."

"Incest pool?" I ask.

"Rumor has it her relationship with her brother is more than it should be," Carmilla says, "it's also said they have the tendency to keep track of their decedents so they can feed off them."

"But if it's a rumor...

Marcus scoffs, "it's not a rumor," he pulls off the pillar, "I've seen it," with that, he walks away. Two other vamps at his heels.

"Is he serious?" I ask.

Carmilla takes my arm and leads me down a hall, "Marcus isn't big on gossip, so if he says it's true, then I believe him."

We make a turn, and then we're down a dimmer hall, "where are we going?" I ask.

"Garage," Carmilla types something into a keypad, and then the door opens, "you get to meet the love of my life," she runs a hand over an expensive-looking car, "this is Ben, the last Bugatti ever made."

"I'm going to assume Bugatti is a brand," around the year two thousand twenty-four major companies officially collapsed, so many name brands lost it all.

"Yup," she pats the roof of her car, "get in."

While fast, the car isn't as fast as Marcus's running; I wonder if I can run that fast. The city, even in ruin, still has a distorted beauty to it. I suppose it could be worse, like in New York, where all their towers fell, or LA, where the fires consumed everything in their path until people had no choice but to move elsewhere.

We stop outside an old building; various shops line the two floors inside. Fake plants adorn the entrance to a shop selling jewelry.

"I thought malls were gone," I say as we pass a stall with tiny figurines.

"This place is immortal run," Carmilla leads me towards a boutique with two intertwined serpents as its logo.

"Carmilla," an exquisite-looking female rushes over, "why didn't you call," a snake wraps around her shoulders, its head resting in one of her hands, "and who's your friend?" The female looks me over, the snake in her hand, hisses, "don't worry, Sari doesn't bite."

"Drishika, this is Lilith; she requires your services," Carmilla walks past her and starts looking through the clothes on a rack.

Drishika moves towards me with a smile on her beautiful face, "tell me, is there any style you prefer?"

"Not really," I take my coat off and set it on one of the lavish chairs.

"Good figure," Drishika nods her approval and heads towards the back. I start browsing through some of the clothes on the rack closest to me.

"What do you think?" Carmilla holds up a black dress with diamonds on the side.

"Fancy."

"But is it proper," she purses her lips, "you see in two weeks Marcus will host the Night of Remembrance."

"Night of Remembrance?"

"It's when we honor our dead," she walks over to another rack and inspects one of the dresses, "I think not."

"Here we go," Drishika returns with a purple and black dress embroidered with silver and a crimson dress with a red lace corset.

"That one," Carmilla takes the crimson dress and drags me into a changing room, "just try it."

The material is soft to the touch; I find the lace has tiny rose patterns at closer inspection. Not only that, but the dress fits like a glove.

"Well?" Carmilla sounds a little anxious.

I step out and walk into a firm chest. When I look up, I find Marcus looking me over wonder in his eyes.

"Don't you agree it suit's her?" Carmilla asks.

Marcus doesn't say anything; instead, he takes a step back and sits next to his sister.

"Exquisite indeed," he finally says.

"Isn't it too much?" I turn to look in the full-length mirror; the dress seems to bring out the red in my eyes.

"You can wear that one during the masquerade," Carmilla says as Drishika hands me another dress.

"When is that?" I ask.

"Winter Solstice," Marcus's eyes travel up and down as if savoring the sight of me.

Careful not to step on the dress's skirt, I step back into the dressing room. The second is a white-collar cocktail dress with a black skirt and white lace bodice. When I step out, both Carmilla and Drishika clap their hands.

"Indeed," Drishika says, "dressing people like her is so easy."

"Like me?" I ask.

"Everything looks good on you," Marcus says, "I need to check on something; stay out of trouble."

"Yes, your Highness," Carmilla snickers. Marcus rolls his eyes at her and gives me a once over, "we'll take them."

"I'll have them delivered," Drishika says, "do you want to try your dress on?"

Carmilla nods, and Drishika disappears towards the back, "I can't afford these," I say, looking in the mirror. I've never worn anything this expensive or lovely.

"Don't worry, Marcus is paying," Carmilla stands behind me and rests her chin on my shoulder, "we should get your shoes before leaving."

Drishika returns with Carmilla's dress and a foot measure. I step back into the dressing room and change into the clothes I came in. Drishika takes the dress and motions for me to sit.

"I just need your foot size," she says, placing the dress inside a black bag labeled S, "I'll have Anuka make the shoes for each dress."

"Anuka?"

"My wife," Drishika says as a lithe female floats over.

"How are you doing that?" I ask.

Anuka smiles while Drishika laughs, "you are new to all of this, yes?" Anuka asks.

"Yes," Carmilla answers as she steps out in an ombre red and white dress.

"It matches your hair," I blur out.

"That was the goal," Drishika says, "I figured I'd play off the feature that almost got you killed."

"Why would her hair get her killed?" I ask.

"I was born during the Salem Witch trials. My mother realized she'd been tricked and tried to hide my pink and white hair," Carmilla says, "one day after my twenty-first birthday, a townie accused me of being a Witch after my coif flew off, revealing I had hair as red as strawberries with streaks of white."

"Wait, how was your mother tricked?"

"She met a stranger there one night gone the next; my guess is he was Fay," Carmilla shrugs, "anyways, as I was about to be burned at the stake, Marcus and Naran swept in and took me away. Naran gave me a choice to become one of the undead or go back and get killed."

"Whose Naran?" I ask as Carmilla steps back into the dressing room.

"He Sired most of us," Drishika says.

"You're a Vampire?"

"I was born a naga, my mother died, and my father tried to kill me, like Carmilla, Naran gave me a choice."

"Our Clan is made up of hybrids," Carmilla steps out in a vintage off-shoulder black cocktail dress, "you are the first mortal turned vampire to join it," she twirls before looking in the mirror, "you are magnific."

"I know," Drishika writes down my foot size and hands it to Anuka, "now hurry and change so I can send everything to the Manor."

"Yes, mother," Carmilla ducks out of the way missing the pillow Drishika throws at her.

"She thinks she's funny," Drishika wipes her hands and stands, "wear your hair up for the Night of Remembrance and no makeup."

"Why?"

Carmilla sets her dresses atop mine, "it's so your loved ones may recognize you."

"Thank you," I say and follow Carmilla out the door, "where are we going?"

"Chose," she points at a salon, then at another clothing store.

I point at the salon; when we step inside, a pixy rushes towards us, "Milla," she twirls Carmilla's hair, "can I play with your hair?"

Carmilla shakes her head and points at me. The pixy lets out a little squill of joy.

"So, pretty," the pixy leads me to a chair; she runs tiny fingers through my hair, the strands turning into red ombre dark on top bright red at the ends. Which, when I look, are no longer split.

"Magic," I whisper as I run my fingers through my hair, "will it last?"

"Of course," pixy smiles, "whenever you want to change it, just come see me," she bobs her little head sideways.

Carmilla places a gold coin on the table in front of me, "the folk don't care for cash or credit cards."

Ah yes, credit cards somehow survived the downturn of the century, unlike cryptocurrency, which like the internet, collapsed. We thank the pixy and head out, stopping at a few shops here and there; by the time we near the food court, I've gotten an entirely new wardrobe.

Taking in all the stalls of food, I ask, "How will I pay him back?"

"What did you do before?" Carmilla asks.

"I helped a midwife and worked at a bakery," I take a bite of the sugary donut Carmilla hands me and stop myself from moaning since when did donuts taste this good.

Carmilla taps her chin, "Anything else?"

"Before that, I used to work at the library, but then it got shut down due to lack of funding," I wait for the doughnut to come back up, but it doesn't.

"Told you," Carmilla finishes her scone and hands me a napkin, "we'll think of something."

"Lilith!" someone shouts my name.

I turn to find Sean and Mika standing there, dumbfounded, "Oh, hi."

"Where have you been?" Mika takes a step towards me, "We were worried."

"Why?" I tilt my head sideways, "did you worry you couldn't poison me anymore, or lie for that matter?"

Mika tries her best to appear hurt by my jeer, "It's not what you think," she protests.

With a sigh, I say, "when someone says it's not what you think, it tends to be so."

Unlike Sean, who snorts, "What would you know?" Mika looks flabbergasted.

I take a step towards him, "more than you'd like."

"Come back with us," Mika pleads.

It seems I've only now realized I can smell their lies, "Rafael said I needed a Clan," I take a step back, "I found one."

Sean laughs, "Of course, you'd pick them."

"Considering this regards my safety," I cock my head to the side, "I'd say they're the better choice, unlike the cesspool Rafael wanted me to join."

"I'm glad to hear," Marcus drapes his arms over Carmilla and me hugging us towards him, "after all, you left quite an impression," the look he gives Sean and Mika would make grown men cry, "are you children lost?"

"You…

Mika stops Sean from speaking, "Lord Marcus, it's lovely to see you."

It seems the cat has a thing for the Lord of the Night, how intriguing.

Marcus gives her a bored look, "can't say I agree," he turns his attention to us, "Now, are you ladies done? I've made reservations."

Rather than pushing Marcus away, I ask, "Where?" Catching a glimpse of jealousy from Mika.

Carmilla laughs, "Your excitement will always amaze me."

Marcus smiles at me, "it's a surprise, don't worry, you can eat till your heart's content."

I turn, taking his arm into my hands, "then what are we waiting for."

Without a second look, I let Marcus lead me away, "don't worry, someone already took your bags to the manor," he sends.

"Stop doing that," I send back.

"No," he gives me a side look. Once outside, we climb into yet another expensive-looking car.

"Carmilla will meet us there," he closes my door and walks over to his side. Once inside, he starts the engine, "thanks for playing along."

"It's always come easily," I lean my head against the window.

"You should be an actress," he says.

I sit up, "Do they even exist anymore?"

"Yup," he makes a turn then stops at a red light, "just because the government has taken over the media doesn't mean acting is dead. Most have gone back to the old ways."

"You do realize the old ways to me have two meanings," I say, "old ways like when my parents were growing up and old ways like when you were first around."

That last remark earns me a flick on the forehead, "I'd argue I'm not that old, but I'd be lying."

Rubbing my temple, I ask, "Whose Naran?"

Marcus tenses a bit, "What?"

"Carmilla and Drishika said you know him and that he Sired them," something makes me want to know more, "is he your Sire to?"

He relaxes his hold on the steering wheel, "Naranbaatar is my uncle. He and my Sire were lovers. She turned me thinking it would please him."

Wow, not what I was expecting to hear. "I take it, it didn't.?"

"Naranbaatar Rurik does not like surprises, and while he had promised his sister to watch over her bloodline. He also promised not to turn any of her descendants unless we asked him to."

A voice whispers in my head, pushing me to ask more. "What happened then?"

Marcus laughs, "Seraphina was persistent in being with him; they had a love-hate relationship," he pauses for a moment, "when she died, Naran lost his mind. No longer carrying for the coven they had founded, he walked into the sunlight, but by then, he was too old to die."

Too old to die? "Wait, you're telling me because he's Ancient, he can't die?"

"I didn't say that," Marcus makes another turn before parking, "the sun, while it bothers his eyes, will not kill him. Now, beheading would kill him, but then again. Who wouldn't that kill?"

He steps out of the car and comes around to open my door, "So, where is he?"

Ignoring my question, he points towards a candlelit patio, "Carmilla doesn't like to wait."

"How did she get here before us?" I follow him inside.

"You made me take a wrong turn," Marcus smiles at the faun before us.

I frow at him, "When?"

"When you asked about Naran," we follow the faun to a table set up next to a fire pit.

Carmilla occupies one of the four chairs set up, "you're late," she says with a small smile.

"My apologies," a male voice resonates from behind me.

"Don't let it happen again," Carmilla rises to greet the stranger, "Eicca meet Lilith."

Eicca takes my hand and kisses my knuckles, "you are enchanting."

I just stare at him; his voice is like rumbling thunder and his eyes, the left one is green and the right ruby.

"How?" I ask, unable to contain my curiosity.

"How are yours like fire?" he asks.

Marcus clears his throat and takes my hand out of Eicca's, "why don't we sit?"

"Old friend, don't worry," Eicca pats Marcus's shoulder, "I already married."

"And what a shame that is," Carmilla winks at me, "don't worry, Eicca, when she grows old and dies, I'll be waiting."
Eicca turns to Carmilla, "that joke is never funny."
I take my seat between Carmilla and Marcus, "she's not serious, is she?"
"Unfortunately, she is," Marcus hands me a menu, "order whatever you like."
"I've spent a lot of your money," I open the menu and avoid looking at him.
Marcus lets out a laugh, "Don't worry, you'll pay it off."

CHAPTER SIX

From what Eicca and the others explained last night, all the clans must listen to a Queen. The question is, is the Queen he referred to, my abuela Reina.

When I was about nine, I had a dream, and, in that dream, my grandparents were Vampires, and my father was a dhampir conceived when my Abuelo was still mortal. Due to my mother's mortality, I was classified as a mortal. Yes, I had speed and strength different from mortals, but I lacked hunger.

Thanks to that, when my parents were murdered by hunters. Abuela decided to send me to my mother's sister. Aunt's daughter had just passed away, so switching our bodies wasn't tricky. Of course, I had to forget for my safety, and Aunt Gethwine had to believe I was Lili.

For whatever reason, all of the forgotten memories came to me my first night at the Sanguis House. Yet, I awoke as if from a deep sleep and brushed it off as if it were nothing. That constant dream since I was nine is now my reality.

I was never insane; the spirits I used to see were not imaginary, and most importantly, I wasn't turned. Now I just need to find my abuela, how difficult can it be?

I crawl out of bed and pad towards the bathroom; my eyes seem to glow; brushing my fangs, I study my features. It seems my eyes aren't the only thing that changed; the scars and blemishes are gone. My features appear sharper, and obviously, my fangs are more extended and sharper.

If my dream was true, would I not be guilty of lying to these people. Of course, so far, they've done nothing to lose my trust, but what if it's all a façade. Should I tell them my theory, for I don't believe I was initially mortal, to begin with? Would they kick me out, although if this clan consists of hybrids, perhaps not? But if my dreams are true, how can I find my abuela?

Too many questions and not enough answers, I head towards the cafeteria, stopping just outside the threshold as I realize I have no money; how will I get food.

"Either go in or move out of the way," a male with onyx eyes says.

"Sorry," I say, stepping to the side. What should I do?

"Lil," Carmilla approaches, followed by a small group consisting of Vincent, Luis, and a female I've yet to meet, "why haven't you gone in?"

"I'm not that hungry," I lie.

Vincent snorts as he walks past, "Liar."

"Don't mind that rude child," Carmilla takes my arm and leads me into the cafeteria. Long tables are arranged to form a giant rectangle, and servers are busy bringing out food. Marcus sits at the center of one of the tables, several empty chairs next to him.

"And you complain about my punctuality," Marcus remarks as we take our seats.

Vincent appears with a plate loaded with bacon, eggs, glazed donuts, strawberries, and pineapple. He takes a bite of bacon, a wicked glint in his eyes.

"Is he truly mortal?" I ask, Carmilla.

She looks over at Vincent, a sad smile on her face, "he is."

Marcus clears his throat as he stands with a glass raised, "tonight marks the start of the Night of Remembrance. After tonight do not overindulge; remember we must not feed for the next seven nights. For on the eight, we feast."

The entire dining hall erupts into cheers as Marcus takes his seat.

"Why seven days?" I ask as a plate of food is placed before me.

"That's how long our ancestors held out during the Immortal Wars," Carmilla takes a bite of a tiny chocolate tart. "On the Eighth night, they won the war but not without a few losses, so on the night it all began we feast as the warriors of old did for once the war began, they did not eat until the Eight night."

"Did you fight in that war?" I ask around a mouth full of bacon.

"The greater majority of those present fought," she smiles weakly, "basically anyone over three hundred has fought in the Immortal Wars."

"You're three-hundred?" I can only imagine the things she's seen.

She takes a sip of wine before answering, "I'm three hundred and seventy-four; guess how old Marcus is?"

"I don't know a thousand," I take a sip of wine, the fruitiness complementing my bowl of berries.

Carmilla laughs, "your kind of close; he's five hundred and forty-five," she winks at the glaring Marcus.

"Then how is he your brother?" I take a bite out of a steamed bun of spicy pork, making my mouth water.

"It's the hierarchy Naran established," she says, "since Marcus and I are not that far in age for a very long time he had us play at siblings when living amongst mortals," she takes a bite of melon, "Naran was always our uncle."

"So, it just stuck," I say as my plate gets taken away. I seem to have finished my food without realizing it. A glass of blood is placed before everyone except Vincent. Marcus raises his glass as if saluting the heavens and all follow suit before downing the glass of blood.

Flames rise from the center of the ground; it seems the tables were placed around a pit of fire; "Let the flame burn until our ancestors return home," Carmilla proclaims as she throws the empty glass into the fire.

I doubt my ancestors fought in their war, so would they return home?

CHAPTER SEVEN

Everything hurts, but I need to get up; after eating, Marcus dragged me into the workout room built atop the roof of the manor. There he proceeded to test my reflexes, leading to me lying face up into the clouds. My body feels like it's been tossed down a flight of stairs, followed by the crushing pain of being buried under a pile of stones. Marcus is simply too strong, too ruthless.

"Get up," Marcus commands as the clouds part the moonlight illuminating him in silvery light, making him seem like a Deity of War. So much hard muscle yet not too much to make you puke, "Lilith!" my name a command, a summons I hoist myself to my feet, barely managing to stand as my leg has yet to finish healing.

Rubbing my aching leg, I ask, "Could you be less rough?" I try to balance myself on my right leg.

Marcus snarls, "Vincent could do this at the age of eight, and he is a mortal," his eyes glow with hunger, "perhaps the little mortal is stronger than a Vampire."

"You gave me no warning but preceded to bounce me off the wall like a bouncy ball!" I shout as I feel the bones in my left leg complete the healing process.

"Do you think, on the battlefield, your enemy will give you a warning?" Marcus asks just as Eicca walks in.

Eicca seems like heaven-sent salvation at that moment, "I'll take it from here," Eicca says in greeting, "go handle your Clan's affairs."

Marcus storms out without a word; the two guards always follow him.

"Are you going to toss me against the wall, then beat me to a pulp and get pissed when I can't keep up?" I ask as Eicca leans down to examine my leg.

"You must understand we were bred for war," Eicca takes a step back, "we had to learn fast or risk death. Marcus was born a Prince descendant of warriors failure was never an option what he just did to you is nothing compared to what he went through when he first learned to walk."

"You know him that well?" I ask, realizing I am to copy Eicca's movements. Back straight arms reach the sky as if in prayer, then down again.

"He's the one that turned me right after he drove his sword through my chest," Eicca points at the scar above his heart.

I look at him with wide eyes, "how are you, friends?"

Eicca laughs, "he said it would be a shame to lose a sparring partner."

"Then they fell in love and had many beautiful babies," Carmilla laughs, "I can't help myself."

Eicca snorts, "I've never understood your sense of humor."

Carmilla winks at me before taking Eicca's arm and flipping him over her shoulder, "if you haven't figured it out by now," she stands up straight as if examining a masterpiece, "you never will."

Training with Carmilla and Eicca isn't any better. By the time I return to my room, I feel as if my body has been broken and rebuilt multiple times. Whoever said Vampires didn't feel pain lied even my hair hurts.

I soak in the tub until I drift off to sleep this time; I'm standing atop the tallest building in Chicago long before it collapsed, and a voice tells me to jump; it will all be fine; only when I jump do I wake up. Where I still mortal, the water would probably feel cold, but as I'm not, whatever temperature change has occurred does not affect me. The voice from my dreams hunts me all the way to the stacks that make up the library.

The voice reminded me of the night I was sent to live with Aunt

Gethwine. It was a voice as sweet as honey yet commanding as thunder Abuela always had that effect. Aunt Gethwine had stood atop the hospital roof, ready to jump when Abuela found her. Per my mother's request, Abuela had kept an eye on Aunt. Unfortunately, we were too late to save the real Lilith, yet Abuela saw it as an opportunity to erase Chrysanth Nightshade. After all, what better way to keep someone hidden than to pass them off as dead, and so Abuela erased Aunt Gethwine's memories, making her believe the one that died that night was her niece and not her beloved daughter.

"What are you doing here?" Marcus's voice pulls me back to reality; apparently, I walked face-first into a wall and didn't even notice.

I look into emerald eyes filled with hunger with wrath, "I needed to clear my mind."

Marcus inhales, looking away as if regretting the action, "the sun should have claimed you; how are you awake?"

What an odd thing to ask, wasn't he awake as well, "how are you awake?" I retort.

His eyes become slightly unfocused as if something were not quite right with him, "I've lived far longer than you," is all he says, staggering as he takes a step back.

I set the book I was holding on the nearest shelf and walk towards him, "are you alright?" there seems to be a glint of madness in his eyes.

Marcus curls his lip back, "don't come near," he commands through gritted teeth.

Too bad for him I'm not very good at following orders.

Marcus snarls with every step I take towards him, even as a child, when approaching a feral beast; it always sends a kind of thrill through me. I clasp the front of his shirt with my hand, accidentally tearing a button off.

The smell of blood engulfs him, "If you cannot feed," I ask, pressing my body closer to his, "why would you go get yourself hurt?"

Marcus tenses as I run my tongue over the hornets, sting the hole the size of a peach. His blood makes my own sing the taste as delectable as the finest of wines.

"Lilith," Marcus's voice is hoarse as he calls out my name, "stop."

I pull back only so I can look him in the eye, "no," I dig my nails into his shoulder as I inch even closer, wanting to lick the blood off his throat.

Marcus trembles in my arms, "do you know what you are doing?" he asks.

In response, I run my tongue over his jaw, nipping just enough to not break the skin. His arms wrap around me, and suddenly I'm sprawled atop a bed of dark velvety sheets.

"I'll ask you one last time," he lets his shirt drop as I prop myself up with my elbows, "Is this what you want?"

"At least for tonight," I lift my gown over my head exposed entirely to him, "just for tonight," I repeat as he sinks his fangs in the motion sending a drilling chill through my being. I've only ever done this once before, and I have to say it does not compare.

Even without the blood-drinking the way Marcus moves, the way my body reacts not once during that first time did, I feel such a delicious thrill. My body responds in ways I did not think possible, wanting to see just how much further things can go. The sunsets, the blinds rise, and we remain a mixture of feeding and fucking, while a voice not my own screaming in anger somewhere deep within my subconscious. At some point in time, we fall asleep, and for once, I do not dream. I do not fear.

CHAPTER EIGHT

"H ave you lost your damned mind?" Is the scream that wakes me, followed by "Silence."

I keep my eyes closed, waiting to see what else I'll hear.

"Marcus, you know if Naran learns we have her let alone that you claimed her, he will end us all," that voice sounds like Carmilla, "what the hell were you thinking?"

"He wasn't," Eicca interjects just how many people are in this damned room.

"It was her choice," Marcus finally speaks; he sounds worn out as if he hadn't slept, "I only complied as I have done life afterlife."

"And where has that gotten you?" Carmilla's tone is as acidic as venom, "each lifetime Naranbaatar awakens and kills her. Why should this time be any different?"

"Because this time, while he may have sired her, he already left her for dead," Marcus says, "didn't he leave her in a ditch?"

"Even so," Eicca doesn't finish his sentence. Instead, Marcus's voice whispers in my head, "you could simply join us."

"With a house this big, you had to chat here?" I sit up feeling as if my body were lighter.

"Your readjusting," Carmilla hands me a robe.

"Readjusting to what?" I ask, rotating my shoulders as I stand silver hair falling down my shoulders, "what?"

"You consumed a great deal of Marcus's blood," Eicca seems

slightly sympathetic, "whatever it is you were before being turned reacted to it, and your body had now undergone a new change."

I look around the room, "What do you mean?" Marcus sits with his head tilted back, eyes closed, his skin slightly ashen. "What happened to him?"

It's Carmilla that answers, "you did."

I halt my hand mid hair hovering above Marcus's head, "I don't understand."

"You drank way more than he could afford to give," Eicca stretches a blood bag towards Marcus, "he's refusing to feed."

"Why?" I take the bag and try to press it against Marcus's lips, "just drink."

"Did you forget we are not to feed or overindulge for the next seven days?" Carmilla asks, "Marcus will not die, but he won't be able to function as he should."

"With Marcus entering dormancy, Carmilla must take over the House as acting Leader until Marcus can rejoin us," Eicca takes the blood bag and tosses it into a cooler. "Since you are the reason Marcus is now in this state, you will help Carmilla."

Without thinking, I blur out, "who died and made you king? giving out orders like you're in charge."

Eicca leans down to my eye level; all pleasantness is gone, "Currently, Marcus is as good as dead. Are you strong enough to guard his body? Had you not bled him dry, would any of this be necessary?"

Carmilla pushes Eicca to the side, "these are the rules established long ago. We ever only have to use them whenever you are reborn."

I'm moved to the side as Marcus is laid down to rest atop the bed. The curtains tied to each bedpost are undone, hiding his body behind them.

Carmilla drags me out of Marcus's room and towards my own, "Unfortunately, the entire house is aware of what you've done."

"How would they know?" I ask, still trying to figure out what Eicca meant by rebirth.

"Marcus announced my appointment," Carmilla says, "he was originally going into dormancy until his wound healed, but you've always been his weak point."

CHAPTER NINE

This again, "Could you elaborate, or am I to guess?" I can feel the anger starting to rise.

Carmilla takes a seat at the edge of the bed and says, "Over a thousand years ago, you walked this earth as the mother of the Undead and Forsaken. It is believed that from you, most immortals came to being. You made the mistake of falling in love with a mortal, and your betrothed, chosen by gods, knows who murdered him in a fit of rage."

I must be looking at Carmilla like she's gone mad, for she says, "just listen until the end." I let myself slump onto the bed as she continues, "Eight times you found each other and eight times you were torn apart by greed and jealousy, so you threw the world into chaos by creating all creatures of the night or at least most."

"How do you know this?" I ask as such a story belongs in books of fable.

Carmilla looks me in the eye as she says. "Because I was the one who betrayed you," there is only sadness in her eyes, "I thought you had fallen upon the wrong path as our kind at that time had it forbidden to enter any kind of relationship with mortals. It wasn't until I betrayed you that I realized my mistake. Eicca and Marcus were half-brothers, with Eicca being what some, later on, came to call a demigod, he hated you for the death of his brother, but when he learned, I lead to your downfall, he learned to despise me."

"Why?" I ask, fighting the urge to simply collapse. The more Carmilla speaks, the heavier my head feels.

"Why to what part?" Carmilla asks as blood tears fall down her face.

"Why did you even tell him?" I want to scream that nothing she is saying makes any sense. I know in my heart there is some truth to her words.

Carmilla wipes away the tears leaving red smears across her lovely face.

"In the beginning, I didn't love Eicca," Carmilla whispers, "I thought if he came to hate me, I could be free."

How did this go from being a god to Carmilla's sad love story?

"The heavenly realm had decided Eicca, and I would be bound," Carmilla sighs as if her soul were tired. "Unlike you, I wasn't brave enough to take what I wanted, let alone fight for who I loved."

"I did what you couldn't," I say more to myself than her, so she to loved a mortal.

Carmilla smiles, but there is no happiness in her smile. "Yes, I too loved a mortal, but I was told our love was wrong, and so Selene was burned at the stake." The look she gives me says it all. It wasn't that she was jealous; no, Carmilla didn't want her ending to be my own. Yet, in seeking help from my betrothed, she ended up dooming us all.

I lean over and hug her; perhaps being betrayed in the past has made it so I can tell when someone is telling the truth and when they wish to make me a fool. Carmilla, in this lifetime, was the first person to tell me the truth, for even as a child, I could tell there was something my grandparents weren't telling me.

I don't let go of my hold until Carmilla does, "You need to sleep," she tries to hide the fact she's still crying.

'I'm not tired," I reach my hand out and start to rub her back like you would a baby's aching belly. We sit in silence for some time, but I do not mind. It seems even as gods; we were not allowed to live our lives as we pleased.

Carmilla falls asleep before the sun even beings to rise. I tuck her into my bed and make my way towards the building's training room on the roof. I want to see if the sun will really burn me. With my eyes closed, I stand on the edge, head held high if the sun burns me, then let it be my end, but if it doesn't, let it be their end. I do not need to guess to know the one that turned me was Naranbaatar Rurik, nor do I need to speculate why my Abuela did what she did. For Reina, Nightshade never did anything without reason. The sun begins to rise, its rays sending a chilling warmth throughout the morning. As the sun continues to rise, I open my eyes; yes, the light is somewhat bothersome, but I do not burst into flames. There is not a single blemish on my skin.

The day I was taken to Heather's house, her children, if not herself, must have cast some sort of spell triggering the sunburn I received that day. Just like poison was mixed into the spiced blood I drank that day.

I wonder if there is a way to regain my memories just like Carmilla has managed to retain her own.

The scent of lavender and honey fills the air around me like a welcoming cocoon followed by that of rose and peony. I don't need to look to know they have finally come for me.

CHAPTER TEN

My grandparents are as eternally youthful as they were in my childhood. The sun makes it seem as if Abuela's eyes were ablaze. While Abuelo still seems like a magnificent giant towering over Abuela like some guardian angel sent by the underworld.

"Mi querida Chrysanth, cómo as crecido," Abuela exclaims.

Abuelo smiles as he engulfs me in a hug, "My love, Chrysanth still seems little to me."

"Corazón mío," Abuela places a slender hand on Abuelo's arm, "en comparación a ti todos somos pequeños."

I laugh for what would be the use in crying.

Abuelo lets me go just so he can pick up his wife, "you're the one that chose me," he plants a kiss atop her brow.

Abuela clicks her tongue, "when have I ever complained?" she gives him a quick kiss before he can respond, "Have you forgotten? It is your height; I found the most alluring your eyes came second to your voice, and then everything else followed."

That's right, Abuela and Abuelo met at one of his shows back when he was mortal. She loved watching him on stage as much as she did, listening to his singing that she decided he would be her groom. So, one night after their last show in Europe, Abuela chose to abduct him the way Vampires of old used to do to young maidens and gave him two options die or be her eternal lover. To Abuela's surprise, Abuelo had become infatuated with her and had no problem with her request.

That's not to say others didn't object; after all, when Abuela was turned, it was very much so against her will. When she came to, she found herself in a strange room with three men, if you could call them that. The Vampire that sired her had fallen asleep atop her, so she bit his throat out. The werewolf and werecat added to her unique existence tried to take her down. Still, when the last one realized his mistake, Abuela was already dangling his intestines before his eyes. She walked out of that shithole drenched in her captors' blood.

It is not just Vampires that have to kneel at Abuela's feet but all immortal creatures that walk this earth. There wasn't a soul that didn't want to claim her to tame and break her. So, Reina, Queen of Vampires, did the only sensible thing that could come to mind. She hunted down every last immortal who insisted on trying to break her and ended their miserable lives. Actually, that is the only truth Abuela ever told me.

"Foolish child," Abuela chides, "why couldn't you just go along with the original arrangement? I no, we did all of this so you could be free."

This is the second truth she's told me, "I did not mean for any of this to happen," I look her in the eye as I speak not doing so could result in a scolding at best at worst a beating, "but I must ask, how did you know what and who I am?"

"After her turning, Reina regained the memories erased by the water of lethe along with her original powers." Abuelo offers as an explanation, "the moment you were conceived, Reina could tell whose soul had been selected for rebirth and did everything she could to make your life better this time around."

This is Abuelo's first truth; how odd it is to be able, to tell the truth from lies.

"But why would you care?" I feel there is more to this story but will they tell me is the question.

Abuela places her hand atop my crown. "Because my sweet child, I too was once a Deity in another time in another world." Her smile is as happy as it is sad, "I too ended worlds for what I believed to be right; I too was oppressed by a gender whose greatest pain is getting kneed in the balls. By a gender that is used to taking from us as they please when they please."

Before I can point out how she did end up choosing a male mate, Abuela says, "once upon a time you would have had to call your Abuelo, Abuela. We do not choose the vessel we are born into. Yet, for some, it seems to become their whole identity. So much so they chose to oppress that which they once were."

Abuelo seems a little sad as the sun reaches its apex, "it's time," they say as one, "our Empire will now be yours," Abuela winks as they start to turn to stardust, "reclaim that which is yours," are her parting words as the wind carries them away to heavens knows where.

I feel waves of energy coursing through me as I feel my head split open, and a flood of memories overwhelms me. Collapsing to the ground, I cradle my head in my arms as I curl into a ball. Gods above, gods below. What in damnation is all that I'm seeing, all that I'm feeling.

PART TWO

CHAPTER ELEVEN

Not only did I miss the Night of Remembrance, but I also missed the Winter Solstice and was once again declared dead. While I didn't get to wear either of the dresses, Drishika had made for those nights, I assume she created my burial gown. I had awakened to yet a new change in the world. During my slumber, the world had a reset, as if the chaos that plagued us for the last couple of years had never existed.

For whatever reason, I was buried on Sanguis land but not within the Sanguis walls. It's such a shame; the gown was ruined as I dug myself out.

"Nice costume!" a stranger dressed as a fake Dracula shouts.

What in the hell? Ignoring the stranger, I continue towards the Sanguis Manor, where no soul is in sight. I step inside to find everything, not as I recall. It's as if the Manor had been abandoned cobwebs cling to the walls, the stairs, and just about anywhere they can get to. Where did everyone go?

As I walk throughout the Manor, I find everything looks outdated, like this place hasn't been touched since the nineties. The electric blinds Marcus had installed are gone, and in their place are boring old curtains that have seen better days. The library is as dusty as the rest of the house, but hardly any books are left. How is it possible they all up and went and why?

"I think this place could be of some use," a familiar voice says, "what do you think, Uncle?"

I move towards the sound; two men stand at the foyer's entrance. Marcus looks so different from when I last saw him, and the one next to him, even though his back is to me, makes my skin crawl.

"Will you come out and greet us?" the stranger with hair as white as snow asks, "or will you continue to eavesdrop?"

I approach with the caution of a cat waiting for its chance. The stranger turns, ruby-red eyes greeting me. Naranbaatar Rurik stands before me, dressed in a suit of purest black.

"And who may this enchanting creature be," Naranbaatar walks towards me with a smile that would be considered attractive if I didn't find him repulsive.

I move out of reach, bumping my back onto a familiar chest, "Marcus," I don't take my eyes off Naranbaatar as I ask, "where did you go?"

Marcus's breath caresses my skin as he asks, "have we met?"

As his arms wrap around me, I spin around, "How could you forget? Did Naran do something to you? Where's Carmilla?"

Marcus's emerald eyes shimmer like stars but don't seem to hold any recollection.

Just as I'm about to ask him if he's alright, Carmilla walks in, followed by Luis, "I think this place could work?" Our eyes lock as she comes to stand by Naranbaatar, "Brother, I see you finally got yourself a bride?"

Marcus takes my arm and twirls me around, "Is this your doing?" he tightens his grasp and shakes my arm mid-air, lifting me up like a ragdoll.

Carmilla pouts; not a trace of the sadness she felt last I saw her seems to remain. "Why is it you always find the need to blame me for everything. Is she not the girl you enamor all those years ago?"

What in the world is she talking about? Before I can speak, I hear Carmilla's voice in my head, "just play along; no one else will believe you."

"But you do?" I send back.

"I'll explain later," she sends, "just get Marcus to acknowledge you."

"How come only sister Milla remembers me?" I look at Marcus as if he'd broken my heart, "how could you forget the three nights we spent together?"

Marcus looks as if I'd struck him, "madwoman, I have never met, let alone touched you."

"I see how it is," I take hold of his shirt, the action familiar, "now that you've gotten what you wanted, you think you can get rid of me. You promised to love me for all of eternity," I try to shake him, but he doesn't budge; I suppose when I could move him before had more to do with him being poisoned than my actual strength.

"I said I've never met you," Marcus tosses me to the side as if I were nothing to him.

"If we had never met?" I hoist myself up and don't bother to hide my annoyance, "how would I know you have a birthmark in your inner thigh close to your...

Before I can finish the sentence, Marcus has his hand around my throat, squeezing so that I may not speak. "Enough!"

I claw at his hand were I not a Vampire; I would probably feel like I'm suffocating; the problem is the action is simply annoying and somewhat painful. "Do something." I send to Carmilla.

Carmilla rushes over, "Marcus put her down," she tries to pry his hand off my throat. Marcus applies more pressure which starts to make me somewhat dizzy.

"Just let her be your maid," Naran's command causes Marcus to loosen his grip.

Carmilla kneels down beside me, inspecting Marcus's handy work, "thank the Underworld you aren't mortal."

"Perhaps if I was mortal, Marcus would care," I rub at my sore throat, the action adding to the discomfort, "what century is this?"

Carmilla looks a little confused as she says, "20th century, why do you ask?"

 I point at Naranbaatar, "that one wants to make me a maid. For a moment, I thought Marcus would kill me, and I'd time-traveled to the Middle Ages."

Carmilla chuckles, "silly girl, time travel, I think Marcus strangling you has affected your brain."

Something keeps me from saying my brain is just fine, but considering I'm apparently in the 20th century, perhaps my brain isn't processing things correctly.

CHAPTER TWELVE

Carmilla convinced Naran and Marcus to let me stay in the Manor. Unfortunately, I have to live the life of a maid for an overbearing bastard. The current Marcus is far more different than the one from my period. Even though I only knew Marcus for a few days, he didn't trigger the urge to throttle him. This Marcus is as demanding as the high society ladies Abuela used to tell me about.

Carmilla explained that she is the only one with memories of her past life; thus, the possibility of time travel is not farfetched to her. She explained that telling Marcus who I really am could affect the feature and that, for the time being, I should not reveal my real name to him. I wonder how badly the feature would be affected; it's not like my original period was that great. Besides, Marcus and the others didn't know my real name.

I scrub at the floor, cursing Marcus when I hear, "Who sired you?" being asked by the very devil.

With a growl and a sigh, I bare my fangs at him, "if I told you, would you still treat me like a slave?"

Marcus arches a brow as he crosses his arms and leans against the now clean wall, "if you were truly an Ancient, you'd know this is not how a slave is treated."

I throw the rag I'm holding at his face and kick the pail of water at him, "what would you call this?" I rattle the enchanted chain around my neck meant to track my every movement, "to add to it, you have me cleaning the fucken floor on my fucken knees with a bloody rag. Have you people never heard of a mop or vacuum?" I tear off the wet end of my maid dress, leaving most of my legs exposed.

"Vulgar creature," Marcus throws the wet rag on the floor.

"Vulgar is this damned dress you have me in," I shout as I tear off the sleeves, "in case you haven't heard, this is the twentieth century, and in only a few months, it'll be the twenty-first century, so I suggest you get used to seeing females walking around with their fucken knees exposed." I storm off before he can give another one of his lectures. For the last two weeks, Marcus has taken every chance he has to get under my skin, and I have to say so far, it's working.

Why the hell would I end up in this cursed period? While Marcus continues to be the bane of my existence, Naranbaatar pretends to be ever carrying, offering things I have little to no care for.

"Why are you following me?" I turn to face Marcus just as the sun starts to rise, its warmth engulfing me in its embrace, "If you truly didn't wish to be with me, why imprison me here?"

Marcus seems to be entranced by something only he can see. I turn my gaze behind me but find only the sun greeting me. Perhaps he's crazy in the head.

"You're able to stand in the sun without burning," Marcus reaches his hand out, running a finger down my chin, "how?"

I must be looking at him like he's stupid because he adds, "how are you standing in the sun? Only hybrids can do that and Ancients."

"My father was conceived shortly after my Abuela was turned. He was half-vampire, werewolf, and werecat, with just enough tinge of mortal," I say careful not to mention my Abuela will be his Queen in the near out feature, "I was born this way," I raise a hand for emphasis, "just like you are not fully vampire neither am I."

I smack his hand away and walk closer to the roof's edge. Since I'm a vampire, I wonder if I jump and temporarily die, would the cursed chain around my neck disappear.

"What are you doing?" Marcus asks as I balance myself on the ledge.

I turn so my back is to the sun our eyes lock as I say, "setting myself free," I let the wind guide me down the impact splinting my ribs, heavens that hurts. Unfortunately, the fall didn't kill me even temporarily. As my ribs heal, I drag myself into the shrubbery leaning my head back; I close my eyes and sleep.

Since arriving in this period, I've struggled to sleep, an ailment I've never had before.

Cursed be I. I wake to the comfort of silky sheets. Why didn't I crawl further? I reach for my throat, feeling the chain's pressure no more. When I run my fingers over the now smooth flesh, I find the chain gone.

"You shouldn't be so dramatic," Marcus lays next to me with his eyes closed. Looking at him like this makes me want to reach out, but I know better. This is not my Marcus.

"If you were a prisoner, would you not do everything you could to be free?" I ask as I roll to my side. I prop my left hand under my cheek and sigh, "what game are you playing at?"

Marcus rolls onto his side, our breaths mingling as he says, "At least one of us should be free."

CHAPTER THIRTEEN

For a moment, I thought Marcus had changed to the being I knew in my time, but alas, that was a fools' dream. While I no longer have to wear the cursed chain, I am to remain as his personal maid. I help him dress, cursing when I have to tie the tie. Why would anyone wear such a nuisance?

Marcus reaches up, clasping my hand in his own as he takes the tie, "I'll do it," he gives me a fool's smirk. If you're so great, why don't you dress yourself? I want to ask but bite my tongue. Today he's somewhat pleasant; tomorrow, who knows.

"Will you be needing anything else?" I step to the side and select star-shaped cufflinks.

"Not those," Marcus takes the cufflinks and sets them back on the vanity table, "the stars are only for special occasions," he picks up plain old diamonds, "these should work just fine."

As I help him fasten them, I ask, "what would be considered a special occasion?" The cufflinks are surprisingly easy to fasten on.

Marcus leans down, his lips brushing my ear, "my wedding night." The shiver his breath sends down my spine stops as a thought hits me, "have you ever been married?"

He halts his hand outstretched towards the door, "once long ago."

After Marcus leaves, I stay in his, or should I say, our room in hopes of avoiding Naran. Since I am now Marcus's personal maid, I no longer need to do menial work. Instead, my only job is to tend to his every need for a year, and only a year then I will be free. But being free would mean going back to my time for as long as I remain in this period, I will be a prisoner.

I head out hoping to find Carmilla; she had promised to help me out yet has avoided me for a greater part of my stay here. When I see her, Carmilla gives the construction workers instructions on how the library should be expanded upward.

"We need to talk," I say in a manner of greeting.

Carmilla smiles as if her smile could hide the fact my presence annoys her. How could she be the most pleasant back home, yet now she's worse than Marcus.

"Unfortunately, I'm currently too busy," she starts shuffling papers as if she were looking for something, "perhaps another time."

"Either we talk now, or I find Selene's reincarnation and end her," I yank the papers out of her hand, "the choice is yours."

The look Carmilla gives me makes me think if she were mortal, her face would be beet red. I toss the papers onto the work table and walk out. Hopefully, I didn't piss her off enough for her to try and kill me, but I simply cannot, will not be here any longer.

"What is it that you want?" Carmilla demands in the form of an outstretched claw towards my heart, which ends up colliding with a poor tree.

Luckily as a child, I used to watch Abuela train with Abuelo, and so knowing when to sidestep and when to attack are things, I learned early on, so I know how to dodge and how to hit. Before Carmilla can spin around to hit me, I raise my arm and strike her behind the neck. It's a good thing Abuelo was a giant as Abuela was my height when standing next to him, and she proved you don't need to be very tall to knock someone out. Abuela used to say all you need is determination and precision. Then she'd flip Abuelo on his back and press her dagger against his throat; of course, Abuela was always the more bloodthirsty of the two.

I drag Carmilla's body into the shrubbery; sitting cross-legged, I place her head on my lap. Closing my eyes, I set a hand on either side of her head. Even though I had been classified as a mortal, Abuela taught me everything a newborn vampire should know;

she'd say, "un día todo podría cambiar." Well, Abuela was rarely ever wrong as everything did change. I head dive into Carmilla's subconscious careful not to leave a trace of my trespassing behind. We all have walls we build to protect ourselves, and in most immortals' cases, those walls are pretty literal.

Carmilla's mind is like a maze made of granite, flames, and wind, every turn more complex than the last. I need to find a way to go forward in time. But for whatever reason, Carmilla has been avoiding me.

CHAPTER FOURTEEN

Diving into Carmilla's mind took up more energy than I had presumed. While Carmilla believes I have traversed time and space, she has decided it'd be best if I never returned to my time. Her reason being so long as I'm around Naranbaatar acts somewhat sensible primarily because Naran wishes to bleed me dry and absorb my essence to increase his power. When Naran is in transition, he will be vulnerable, thus making it easier to kill him. But I wonder what would occur if I were the one to bleed him dry.

I'm sure killing Naranbaatar would result in an alteration to the fabric of time. Perhaps my being sent back to the past served a purpose. If I could end Naran in this time, then the night I was turned would have never occurred, but would killing him change anything else. I could try and find my Abuela in this period, but she is currently a mortal child of about five to six years of age, if I'm not mistaken. What use would it be to find her? Although I could warn her about the night she was turned, would she even believe me, let alone remember.

Ahh, this is all so taxing. Why did this have to happen? I pull the blankets over Carmilla's sleeping form and exit her room. While she wishes to use me, I still wouldn't leave a female unconscious and unprotected out in the open, so carrying her to her room seemed sensible.

"Why were you in Carmilla's room?" Naran's voice makes my skin crawl, but if I want a chance at killing him, I suppose I'd ought to play nice.

With my head held high, I walk up to him and place my hand on his arm, "I wanted to learn how to control my feeding better, and Carmilla said you'd be the one to talk to. Luckily, you are before me, and I don't have to hunt you down."

If Naran doubts my lie, he doesn't let it show, "how have you not learned control?" he plays with a strand of my hair as white as his own.

I lift my hand up, clasping his in my own, "my sire wanted to die at the loss of his lover," I look down as if sad, then chew my bottom lip while pretending to contemplate whether or not I should continue.

"Speak, child," Naran's voice is a command.

I look up, still chewing over my lip, "he let me drink from him until nothing remained by the time, I came to he was no more than ash," I look away once more before adding, "I haven't feed since, his blood has sustained me until now, but I fear if I feed again, I won't be able to stop."

Naranbaatar gives me a Cheshire cat's smile, his ruby eyes glowing with anticipation, "I will guide your feeding," he drags me into what seems to be the main bedroom and throws me onto an ivory chaise.

Naran removes his overcoat and undoes the buttons of his shirt before removing his cufflinks.

"How is this guiding?" I prop myself up, and Naran plops himself down onto the empty space.

With open arms, he gestures for me to come forward. It can't be this easy, can it? Naran reaches over and pulls me on top of him.

"Since I do not wish to die," Naran pushes my hair to the side and brings his face to my neck, taking in my scent. "I'll make sure to get you to stop," he runs his tongue over my clavicle up the side of my throat and onto my jaw, where he nips, breaking enough of the skin for droplets of blood to fall onto his tongue. "Truly divine," he murmurs.

Before Naran can sink his fangs in, I bite him drinking in the power of his ancient blood. Unlike Marcus's blood, Naranbaatar's lacks sweetness; it's purely bitter and sends a sense of uneasy down my spine. Its evident Naran takes pleasure in our current embrace; one of his hands is tangled in my hair while the other is pressed against my hip. Naran lets out a moan of pleasure as I feed off him; you'd think we were having sex. But then again, Abuela used to say blood exchanges were sacred and should not be done with just anyone.

Just as Naran is about to give the command that sings in his blood, Marcus throws the door open fiery furry in his eyes.

"So, this is why you insisted on staying by my side," Marcus pulls me off Naran, his hold ironclad, "you didn't have to lie," he snarls before throwing me into the hall.

I can hear Naran laugh as I try to sit up; I think the bastard broke one of my ribs when he threw me against the wall.

"My dear nephew, what would be so wrong about sharing her, especially when she's more than willing?"

Through my blurred vision, I can see Marcus blocking Naran's path when he makes to come for me.

"Foolish girl," I hear Carmilla's voice as my vision goes black, and I'm lifted up into her arms.

CHAPTER FIFTEEN

I wake to the comfort of Marcus's bed and scent. Perhaps it was all a dream, I tell myself as I snuggle into Marcus's chest pure, delicious muscle.

"Should we tell her you guys aren't alone?" Carmilla's voice keeps my hand from moving further.

"I think she knows," a voice I've only heard once says, "you can open your eyes."

For fucks sake, why did they have to see that?

"So, do you like Marcus or Naran?" that same male voice asks.

I roll off Marcus and hoist myself up; a familiar sweetness in my mouth has me looking at him to ensure I didn't drain him again.

"So, we didn't meet in the past," Marcus proclaims in the form of greeting. The overly bearing smirk he gives me for a moment makes me think I've gone home. Wait, the bastard head dived.

I raise my hand and strike his chest, "how dare you?"

Marcus catches my fist in his hand, "it was only fair," he looks over to Carmilla.

"If she hadn't pushed me away, I wouldn't have done it," I yank my arm free and pull the bedsheets closer. Carmilla stands with her back to the wall, arms crossed, while Luis leans back on one of the side chairs.

"I had my reason," Carmilla says in defense.

I snort," right keeping me in the dark about wanting to use me to kill Naranbaatar is something that only concerns you." I ask Marcus, "and why are we in bed together?"

He lifts a brow, "I feed you, my blood."

"And?" why is he practically naked.

"And you wouldn't let me go," he looks at me as if it were the most obvious reason.

I close my eyes take a deep breath, and count to ten, "why are you still in bed?'

"Because in case you've forgotten, this is my room and my bed," Marcus nips at my earlobe, "now get up; there are things that need discussing."

How I wish to throttle him, Marcus and the others step into a side chamber I hadn't noticed before. Why in the hell am I naked? "Bastard!" I curse out loud as I grab the robe at the foot of the bed.

"Why am I naked?" I demand to know as I walk into the room.

Marcus just rolls his eyes.

"I needed to make sure the broken rib wasn't piercing your heart," Luis says in apology, "if the fractured rib were to be removed from your heart, you would have died, but luckily it didn't even grace it."

"Is that answer enough?" Marcus asks as if to move the conversation along, "or is there more?"

"Why did you stop me?" I walk over to the table they're standing around, the plans for a ballroom sprawled on it.

"Because only a fool would think it'd be that easy to kill Naran," Marcus taps at a spot with an x drawn onto the plans.

"For Naran to die, it has to be on a special night," Carmilla proclaims, "for whatever reason, Naran has always been weakest during the solstice."

"We think it has something to do with Seraphina's death," Luis says, "he betrayed her, so she chose to extinguish her soul for all of eternity."

"So, we wait until the winter solstice," I study the map; it seems they've thought this out for some time, "I will offer myself as his bride; it's the only way he'd share his blood with me again."

I look up to find all three looking at me like I've gone mad, "I need to be the one that ends him," I say, "I'm assuming x marks the spot?"

Carmilla looks a little pained at whatever thought crosses her mind, "correct, the moment he starts to drink your blood, we'll strike him down."

Should I tell them the one being drained of existence won't be me, but Naranbaatar Rurik? Probably not; after all, they haven't exactly been all forthcoming.

"We'll need a witch," I can't risk Naran not dying, "a powerful one."

It is Luis that asks, "why?"

"Because when all goes to hell," I look Marcus in the eye, "I need the Witch to ensure Naran cannot escape."

CHAPTER SIXTEEN

We all set out to play our part with only seven days until the winter solstice. Marcus has exiled me from his bed-chamber. Luis has set out to find a Witch strong enough to contain Naran should things go haywire, and Carmilla has resumed ignoring me, making my life a living hell any chance she gets. I have to say it sure feels real.

At word that Marcus kicked me to the curb, Naran swooped in as if he were my knight in shining armor. I have to say sleeping next to him every night makes me nauseous. To add to it, I have to ensure my mental barriers are strong enough less Naran decides to head dive while I'm sleeping. I sometimes feel like I'm going slightly mad between reinforcing my shields and keeping an eye on Naran. Naran prances into our shared room, followed by a set of very mortal-looking ladies that seem to be in a trance. He commands them to set down what they're carrying before walking over to me. I fight the urge to pull away as he wraps me in an embrace.

"How delectable your scent is," he kisses my throat before running his tongue over my jugular vein.

"What have you brought me?" I ask, in hopes it'll get him off me.

Naran looks as if he were drunk and gives me a fool's smile, "have a look," he points a hand at the pile of boxes and dress bags the ladies had left behind.

The boxes look expensive enough. I'm afraid to look inside; sadly, not a single box bears Drishika's emblem. The first box is a box within a box that holds a set of emerald earrings with a matching necklace. The second box is the same only instead of emerald; it's a set of blood rubies with a matching choker and bracelet ring chains for either hand. It's obvious what Naranbaatar is trying to do. If I chose emerald, I still love Marcus, but if I chose the blood rubies, I'd be his slave.

Setting the jewel boxes down, I open the dress bags. The first dress is white with gold too pure. The second dress has a black skirt with a green vine pattern on the corset. The third dress has a red skirt with a black corset lined with an imprint of roses trapped within spiderwebs.

"I love them," I twirl around and give Naran a kiss while mentally stabbing myself so I won't strike him.

Naran twirls me around, pressing my back against his chest as he traps me in a hug, "Which will you wear?"

"How about I surprise you," I rub my head against his chest; if I choose now, it'll be too obvious, "what shall we do now?"

Curses, why did I ask that Naran tears of my blouse tossing it to the side. Gods above gods below how I detest his touch. The only way to stomach it is to think of the three nights I spent with Marcus. I just have to remember to bite Naran before screaming out Marcus's name. Naran's more ferocious than usual perhaps my scent has given me away, or maybe something else has him preoccupied that he feels the need to take it out on me.

For someone who has lived for as long as he has, Naranbaatar is not very good at sex. Naran seems to only know how to take but not how to give. How in the world did Seraphina ever put up with it?

CHAPTER SEVENTEEN

I sit in the bathtub far longer than necessary; if there were a way for me to scrub my insides clean, I'd do it. I keep telling myself just a few more days, yet these last seven days seem eternal so far. I've never wanted time to fly as quickly as I do now. Not even when the Bruja Mayor did the test to see if I was more mortal than immortal.

"Come to me," Marcus sends through our telepathic link, a link meant only for emergencies.

I rinse off the rest of the soap and hurry to get dressed. There is no need to worry about Naran; every time he attempts to bite me, he grows unconscious and remains that way until the next day. Naran sleeps with a stupid smile on his face; if only I could kill him where he sleeps; the last time I tried, he woke before I could end him; Naran had assumed my uncontrolled feeding of him meant I wanted sex; unfortunately, he gladly obliged. Carmilla insisted it was better than Naran, knowing we plan on assassinating him. I'd like to have her trade places see how much she enjoys it.

Marcus and the others sit in his secret chamber with a hooded figure sitting at Marcus's right.

"You found the Witch," I lower my head in greeting; the amount of power emanating from the hooded female reminds me of Lady Cendy, the Bruja Mayor.

The female lowers her hood eyes like amber great me and a feral smile, "hello, time walker."

Perhaps it is a dream, for I swear Lady Cendy is sitting before me. Lady Cendy rises from her seat, the cloak falling to reveal a very impressive baby bump, "Have we met before?"

"Lady Cendy, it is an honor to see you again," for whatever reason, I cannot take my eyes off her belly.

The Witch chuckles, "it seems you and my daughter are connected."

At her words, I realize the immense power I'm sensing isn't coming from the Witch before me but rather the baby in her belly.

"You're Lady Cendy's mother?" I look the Witch over, how they resemble each other.

"So, it would seem," the Witch extends her hand, "you may call me Magdalena." I take the warm hand she offers; Magdalena's touch is as gentle as Abuela's.

"You look so much alike," I say as Magdalena places my hand over her belly. The baby kicks as if in greeting before returning to its rest.

"She likes you," Magdalena lets go of my hand, but I linger just a few seconds, hoping the baby will kick again, "do me a favor." At my silence, Magdalena says, "don't tell me anything else. I actually like surprises."

I drop my hand to the side, "Okay," I look down at her belly, "isn't it too risky for you?"

Magdalena smiles, "it is my duty as the Bruja Mayor to help this city that has given me a second chance. Especially when your ancestor will help create a better world for us."

"My ancestor?" I ask.

"The child you wish to visit but are afraid to see has a great destiny," Magdalena returns to her seat, "and we all have our roles to play. While it might be dangerous, I must do everything to ensure my child has a better future than I did."

I will not fail you I send to Lady Cendy and my Abuela. I hope that by killing Naranbaatar, Abuela won't have such a tragic beginning into her immortality.

CHAPTER EIGHTEEN

Having seen Magdalena somehow made returning to Naran's bed slightly more bearable. Only six more days, and we would all be free. Even if my freedom might mean my death, I do not care, for anything can be better than this meaningless existence. Naran stirs in his sleep, "Seraphina," escaping his lips here and there; he must have truly loved her.

What I don't understand is at what point did Naranbaatar try to walk into the sun. If I remember correctly, he should have gone mad by now and left to wonder gods know where but instead, he is here, yes, a tad bit insane but still here. Another thing is if they attempted to assassinate him during the solstice, does that mean they failed, and that's why he was able to awaken me in the future. Considering Naran's personality, wouldn't he have killed them? By the time Naran wakes up, I've been going over all of this. The question still remains, why am I here?

Naran presses his face against my neck, inhaling as he asks, "how did you sleep?"

"Fine," I lie, for I have not truly slept since switching to his bedchamber.

Naranbaatar starts to slide his hand up my nightgown when I ask, "Who is Seraphina?" His hand stops on my thigh, nails digging in.

"Who told you that name?" Naran's eyes show fury for once.

Digging my own claws into his arm, I say, "you talk in your sleep, now answer the damned question."

The fury in his eyes turns into panic; what is he afraid of saying, I wonder.

"What else have I said?" Naran digs his nails in deeper. If only he knew the pain, he's causing is what's keeping me grounded.

"You call her name out every night," ignoring his question, I ask again, "who is Seraphina?"

Naran seems to relax as he loosens his hold on my thigh. I push him to the side and slide out of bed for once, letting him see the disgust his mere presence causes. Of course, he assumes the look I'm giving him is due to what he's done and not because I've always detested him.

He comes to where I sit, applying pressure to my bleeding leg, "my beloved," Naran tries to kiss me as if that would make things better. I do my best to appear jealous as I push him away.

"Naran, my patience is running thin." I need to think of a way to get my blood off his hand can't let him taste me. The blood in my veins is something someone like him should never know. The fact that he got to taste a few drops of my blood that day still worries me.

Naran relents as he plops himself down on the opposing chair, "Seraphina was my one and only love," he looks at me as if it were a test; luckily for me, I've been shooting daggers at him for some time now, "that is of course until I laid my eyes on you. Chrysanth, you must understand before you I knew not what love is. The moment you chose me over Marcus was a most joyous occasion."

I snort; I mean, what other chance will I have to simply show my disgust towards him, "you call this love," I raise my hand to reveal an already healing thigh, "and if you no longer love her, why do you call her name every night?"

The truth is, until last night, he hadn't called out to her. I wonder if it could have something to do with the coming solstice? Will he call out her name more ardently with each passing night?

"I met her when I was a boy," Naran offers, "I had just killed a man who thought himself my better. Seraphina was a true creature of the night lovely and truly wicked."

"Go on," I say as if it still wasn't enough to garner forgiveness.

Naran smiles, "Seraphina refused to turn me, but I loved her with every passing day. Then one day, her sire found her we were in the thralls of passion when he tore my heart out."
I find it hard to believe Naran would ever be in the thralls of anything, let alone passion. Odds are she fed of him as they had sex, and so he never truly learned how to please anyone beyond that point.
"So that's when she turned you?" I ask.
Naran shakes his head, "it was her sire that fed me his blood. See, while I loved Seraphina deeply, she never loved me. By the time I was thirty, she had yet to turn me. Uriel said that showed just how much she loved me."
"Then why did she turn Marcus?" I ask before he can continue with his sob story.
Naranbaatar's eyes light up, showing his true form, "That bastard bewitched her! That's why your leaving Marcus for me felt so great. Now he knows the pain I felt when he stole Seraphina from me."
With a deep breath, I stand and walk over to him. With Naranbaatar, everything is a test; I climb onto his lap, placing a hand on either shoulder. Closing my eyes, I pretend I'm kissing Marcus. Naran lets out an approving growl thrusting his hips against my own. It seems this is the reaction he was aiming for.

CHAPTER NINETEEN

At last, the night was almost upon us just one more day, and all this could end. Magdalena had sent via Luis that she still believed I would cease to exist once Naran died by my hand or another. It was nice to have someone feel concerned for my well-being for a change, but nothing could change what needed to be done.

After Naran's sob story to prove his so-called love to me, I suggested that he announce I was his one and only bride on the solstice night. Hopefully, I can kill him so that such a thing may never become a reality.

Thanks to Carmilla stating I needed to undergo a purification ritual the night before the solstice, I got to spend my last night away from Naranbaatar. Of course, he took it to mean I was preparing for our wedding and not his demise.

"Why are you here?" I pour rose petal water over my head as Marcus slips into the bath. Luckily Carmilla took me out of the Manor for my last night in this world.

Marcus leans against the tub's rim, arms hanging from their ends, "I'm here to purify you," he chuckles.

I hit the water with my hand sending water flying towards his face, "more like defile me," I swim closer to him.

Marcus smiles, fangs glinting in the candlelight, "if that's what you want."

With him, it's always about what I want, never about what he needs or wants.

"Erase him from my skin," I say, and he pulls me towards him spinning me in the water so that my back is pressed against the tub's rim and my legs are wrapped around his waist.

At first, all he does is kiss me, and at first, that's all I need, but with every passing second, every touch, every kiss, and nip, I crave more. I do not have to speak for Marcus to give me what I want. Over and over again, not once do I stop myself from screaming his name. This adrenaline spike only he can give me even without the bite, Marcus sends a jolt of delightful pleasure through my being. Now Marcus was a man who had lived centuries and had actually learned how to please someone and because he knew just what to give, I knew just what to give back.

CHAPTER TWENTY

Perhaps had I been mortal, I would have been sore all over, but thanks to Marcus, I felt purified. I sit facing the mirror as Magdalena's witches work on my hair, carefully placing eight enchanted trinkets resembling pins that will turn into daggers once removed.

"You, foolish girl," Magdalena greets, "could you not wait to see him in your time?" She places a diffuser necklace around my throat, masking it with her magic.

"Considering tonight is the night I die," I look up at her, "I regret nothing."

Magda flicks my forehead, "is he really that great?"

"Oh, you have no idea," I catch a glimpse of her acolytes in the mirror. The two girls turn bright red at my words, "unlike Naran, Marcus actually knows how to use that damned thing between his legs." That last part seems to be what does it; the girls burst out laughing, one even fans herself as Marcus walks into the room.

Marcus gives them a smile that would make most swoon. I'm sure the bastard was listening in. Especially as he looks pretty pleased with himself.

"You have done more than enough," Magdalena stops him with a finger pressed against his firm chest.

"That bath you prepared was symbolic, yes?" I take off my robe, revealing a gown as white as snow with red spider lilies adorning the corset. Carmilla got Drishika to design my dress and the rings adorning my hands. If I am to die tonight, I should at least die wearing something I like.

Magdalena turns away from Marcus; the smile she gives me is that of a sad mother, "it was meant to cleanse you for tonight, but since that one," she points a finger at Marcus, "went and added himself into the equation, I know not if it will affect time itself."

I take the obsidian bangle she hands me, "considering when I ended up here," I smile at Marcus, "we had already spent three nights together. I think he was part of the equation from the start."

Marcus smiles like the proud bastard he is, "only three nights, hu?" he rubs at his chin, "I feel I could have done better."

I roll my eyes at him before taking the final piece of my armor for the night, a bouquet made of vervain, nightshade, and white spider lilies disguised as roses of the purest black. The amount of poison I've already ingested should be enough to kill the entire room. Thanks to Abuela, I have immunity to all poisons and venoms. At the peak of the longest night, Naranbaatar Rurik will die, or all be damned.

PART THREE

CHAPTER TWENTY-ONE

As the celebration goes on, I can sense Naran's power weakening. I wonder if Seraphina cursed him or if there is more to the story. Nevertheless, if I must die, so will he. Being Naranbaatar's nature, he insisted Marcus be the one to hand me over as if he were my father. What a sick way to show he's won, simply pathetic.

Magdalena and her acolytes hide amongst the crowd disguised as Vampires least they are found. Luis and Carmilla stand on either side of the makeshift altar with Naran at the center. I take his hand into my own with a plastered smile, rising to stand by his side.

Naran kisses the inside of my palm before turning to face the onlookers.

"Tonight, I will claim this creature as my bride," Naran raises my arm as if he were auctioning me off, "tonight, I will finally have her blood." Naran brings his lips to my throat.

"Not yet," Carmilla sends, "just another minute."

"Well, think of something," I send back to her.

Carmilla clears her throat and steps forward, "Uncle," she places a hand on his shoulder, "is it truly necessary to make such a display?"

Naran hides his displeasure with Carmilla by turning to the crowd, "tell me, esteemed guest, should I or shouldn't I feed from my new bride?"

Before they can answer, the bell chimes once, then twice my fangs are at Naran's throat. The bouquet I've shoved into his mouth. Carmilla returns to her spot on the altar triggering Magdalena's formation. Naranbaatar spits out the bouquet just as I take one of the eight pins out of my hair and stab one into his back, a chain extending from the dagger. Carmilla picks it up as I jab another dagger into his shoulder, and again another chain extends. Luis takes this one.

Naranbaatar attempts to break free, but the daggers, much like myself, are coated in various poisons. Not only that, but Magdalena's magic formation holds him in place. There is a mixture of awe and horror emanating from the crowd. I do wonder how many here wished Naranbaatar dead.

I insert the final dagger into his chest, the chain wraps around him; the others let go of the chains they're holding as they wrap around Naran, the daggers burrowing into Naran. Whispering and old prayer, I take off the obsidian bangle Magdalena gave me. A blade as dark as night appears in my hands.

"What are you doing?" Magdalena's voice holds fear, fear that I will destroy her new source of power.

"What a descendant of Lady Cerin should do," I plunge the blade into Naran's chest, the blade curving into a crescent on my command so that when I pull it out, it repierces Naran's heart on the way out. Flames made of shadows and darkness start to eat at Naran's very soul as I let go of the obsidian blade. The earth shakes the foundation splitting open as it swallows what remains of Naran.

When I came into this time, my head felt like it was being split open, and the things I saw I could hardly believe.

A long time ago, a Deity was sent down to earth to undergo a trial; she found a dying child clinging to its mother's bones. Without her memories or powers, the Deity took pity upon the child and vowed to not let it die. That child lived thanks to the Deity and grew to regard her as his mother; he pleaded the heavens and Underworld to let his mother stay just a bit longer as she lay on her death bed. When the mother's condition worsened, the child, now a man, offered his own life so that his mother may live. The mother smiled and said, "I did not choose wrong."

Her son did not comprehend his mother's words, but since this was the first time she had spoken in a long time, he was ecstatic, thanking the heavens and Underworld for healing his mother. The son watched with amazement as the Deity's skin began to glow; she rose from the bed.

"I have seen many worlds fall at the hands of men," the Deity proclaimed, "and so I will bless your bloodline so that only daughters of daughters be born with immense power as such are the ways of the Underworld."

"Mother," the man looked pained after all he had done for her, "what of my sons?"

"They will be great warriors bound to the moon," the Deity proclaimed, "but shall the world fall into disarray and your children remain partial, a great calamity will befall for generations." With those final words, Deity Cerin parted from the mortal world, and as she did, the man's first daughter was borne blessed with the mark of the Deity, and from her bloodline, I descended.

Naranbaatar was a mistake created my ancestor's brother's descendant. A mistake it seems I needed to fix, for it looks like Naran's existence was one of the many factors that played into the calamities that befell the world.

I do not feel pain as the world begins to fade, and I turn to ash.

CHAPTER TWENTY-TWO

I open my eyes to the sound of birds chirping and children laughing; colorful lights the size of fireflies' hover above my head, the smell of rose and peony bringing back memories of my mother.

"I'm glad you're awake," Ama pats my head as tears stream down my face. I launch myself at her wrapping my arms so tig I feel I might crush her. "We were only gone for a few days," Ama rubs my back in soothing circles, "I thought you liked staying with your grandparents?"

I let go of Ama to look her over; she looks just as I remember. Ama's doe eyes look me over, clearly searching for the cause of my distress.

"Amor!" Apá walks in with a plate of corundas in hand, "if you don't hurry, there won't be any food left."

I jump off the bed and hug him, almost knocking the plate of food his holding out of his hands.

"Well, good morning to you too," Apá greats as I realize one thing.

"Abuela!" my scream scares my father enough that Ama has to catch his plate of corundas.

"What's the matter?" they ask, fear visible in their eyes.

Abuela rushes in her skin weathered with time; she smiles at me, her eyes all-knowing.

"Lo que será, será," Abuela murmurs as she pats my back, "era necessario."

"But now you're old," I protest, "and look at me." Abuelo walks in his height, nowhere near what it was in his youth, "look at Abuelo, he's short now."

Abuelo kneels down with a bemused smile, "and yet," he looks at Abuela, "she has not left me yet."

"Can someone explain?" Ama asks, her worry now annoyance.

Abuela gives Ama a look that says one more word from you, and I'll kick you out, "Little Chrysanth just had a very long dream."

"Apá, what stories did you read her this time?" my father demands to know.

In this new reality, Abuela didn't have to undergo such a horrid transformation. Not only that, but I got my parents back along with a sister I did not ask for. But to my misfortune, I am now eight going on nine. I have to say that going through puberty all over again does not sound at all pleasing.

EPILOGUE

For the last twenty years, I've spent day and night trying to figure out if what I did in the past had any alternative changes. I have searched every place I visited with Carmilla in hopes of finding the folk, vampires, werewolf, anything to tell me it wasn't all a dream. After my grandparents passed away, I was no longer sure if what I lived was real or simply my delusion, as my parents and sister claimed.

What a great fucken restart I got. With my grandparents gone, my parents had me institutionalized with delusion claims. It seems being the only one left with memories of a life that no longer was really fucks with you. Luckily, I was able to get myself out of that place, and Aunt Gethwine helped me get emancipated. While Aunt Gethwine has her quirks, at least she never tried to deem me insane, as my parents were so quick to do.

I stand before Lake Michigan, feet buried in the sand as the waves crash against my ankles.

"What a lovely moon," I whisper, afraid my voice will scare it away. The waves pull back before rushing forward as if the moon were sending them my way. The impact sends me a few steps back, my back hitting against something hard.

"Not as lovely as you," a voice I thought I'd never hear murmurs against the nape of my neck.

I close my eyes, afraid to look; how many times did I think it was him, and how many times was I wrong.

"I think you've scared the poor thing," a playful voice says.

Could it really be them? I take several deep breaths before opening my eyes. With tears streaming down my face, I turn my head to look at Marcus, whose chin rests atop my shoulder while his arms hold me in a tight embrace.

"If you promise not to hit me," Marcus says, all innocent-like, "I promise to let you go."

"No," I take another breath before saying, "don't let me go."

I let my mental shields down and feel as a cool caress enters my mind, "I should have come to you sooner," Marcus murmurs as he spins me around, tilting his head sideways; he slashes at his throat crimson blood seeping out like a bloody cascade. Without hesitation, I drink and drink until he tells me to stop.

Marcus's blood is the sweetest thing I've ever had. I close my eyes and let the darkness claim me.

ABOUT THE AUTHOR

Eva Peony

Chicago Native Eva when not writing can be found reading and binge-watching K- dramas & C-dramas. She is a full time certified Vampire.

BOOKS BY THIS AUTHOR

Between Shadows & Darkness

Red Snow

Vampire Hearts Werewolf Eyes

9 798779 479646